A WIDE BERTH

Casey Jones heads to Acapulco to join the crew of a cruise ship after crew member Tracy Coleman and a passenger vanish into thin air. But what looks like a promotion turns out to be a demotion when Casey discovers she is actually deputy to Pierre Arbour, a man who gives new meaning to the term obnoxious . . . When Casey finds Tracy's cabin wrecked, and blood in the bathroom, she must enlist help from her new shipboard colleagues and some old friends to get to the bottom of the mystery.

STELLA WHITELAW

A WIDE BERTH

Complete and Unabridged

LINFORD
Leicester

First published in Great Britain

First Linford Edition
published 2015

Copyright © 2010 by Stella Whitelaw
All rights reserved

A catalogue record for this book is available
from the British Library.

ISBN 978–1–4448–2269–4

Published by
F. A. Thorpe (Publishing)
Anstey, Leicestershire

Set by Words & Graphics Ltd.
Anstey, Leicestershire
Printed and bound in Great Britain by
T. J. International Ltd., Padstow, Cornwall

This book is printed on acid-free paper

To Captain David Warden-Owen
and his crew for their skill and
seamanship during twenty-four hours
of a gale force nine on an
unforgettable Friday.

My grateful thanks

to

Tanya Whitehurst
Christine Noble
Cruise Directors

Anna Telfer
James Nightingale
Editors

Security Officers
(*names withheld*)

Valerie Bowes and Diana Green
Ian Green and Charles Thomas
Moral Support

Casey's Ten Commandments

- Always listen sympathetically
- Always listen with patience
- Never look bored
- Never discuss politics or religion
- Never mention illness
- Never ask personal questions — even if the passenger offers answers
- Never boast — exude authority and confidence
- Always be tidy
- Always be sober
- Smile

1

Acapulco

'Casey, we're really sorry, but you've got to go. We've booked the flight. It's an emergency. We've no one else to ask.'

'This is my leave. I'm on holiday. You know, the time of the year when you don't do any work.'

'But we need you. There have been a couple of strange things happening.'

'I don't do strange things.'

'Casey, we are depending on you. It'll go down well on your record when it comes to the annual review and assessment.'

★　★　★

I was born with sea legs but not air legs. The long, cramping, fifteen-hour flight from Gatwick to Acapulco had been purgatory, imprisoned in a seat so small that if there had been the instruction to assume the crash position, it would have been physically impossible. My legs had folded themselves into a concertina and were reluctant to straighten. I didn't know if I'd be able to walk off the plane.

It was hot. Mexico was hot. Acapulco was a spectacular bay of sand and sea with a surrounding range of mountains. Every grain of sand sparkled. The sea was molten silver. For a moment I stood outside the airport buildings and drank in the rugged vastness of the mountains in the distance, but there wasn't time for more than a glance. I had to get a taxi to the quayside.

Strange things happening . . .

★   ★   ★

I am a reluctant investigator, though that's not what it says on my passport. They flew me out to join the refitted ship *Countess Aveline* of the Conway Blue Line at a moment's notice. I was supposed to be on leave. There were two reasons. The ship's current entertainment director, Tracy Coleman, had gone missing, as had a male passenger.

The two events did not seem to be connected, though the two missing persons may have met on board. Head Office thought I might be able to shed some acceptable light on the mysteries. Their assumption had been based on pure lucky guesses I'd made on two previous cruises on the sister ship, *Countess Georgina*.

'My job is to run the entertainment side of cruising,' I said when Head Office phoned me at my flat in Worthing. I was standing at my fourth-floor window, looking at my distant sea view. I had only bought the flat for the view. It cost a pound a pebble. 'I'm not a detective. Send in an extra security officer.'

'Casey,' said a soothing administrative voice, hired for just such a role. 'That's exactly what we want you to do, get the entertainment running with style again. Tracy has been missing for four days, and there's a slight air of panic in the emails from the ship. That's why we are flying you out to Acapulco. Is your bag packed?'

'It's always packed.'

I had a wardrobe of creaseless cruise clothes that only took moments to fold into my wheelie suitcase. Some of the dresses were vintage, unique, glamorous; in the evenings, I had to look the part.

*   *   *

The *Countess Aveline* was the oldest cruise ship of the fleet and she had recently been refitted to meet current fire and safety regulations. A couple of sun decks had been added and all sorts of luxuries updated, cabins refurnished and public rooms given a facelift. She was still an elegant ship, only much bigger.

She had a proper theatre for the shows with a low-slung balcony and tiered seating. They could fly scenery, stage a circus. I'd seen photographs and I was impressed. It was part of my job to glide onto that stage and announce the evening shows. It was still two shows a night, first and second seating for dinner, and the endless feeding round in the

Zanzibar Dining Room and the upstairs Boulevard Café.

Aveline Conway had been eldest of the two daughters of grandfather Jordan Conway, who founded the shipping company, Conway Blue Line. Aveline's partner had been Royce Quentin, the famous explorer, and the couple travelled the world. I knew all this because I loved the history of the three *Countess* ships. Each one was different with a distinct style, but all the ships had that elegant bow line and sweeping hull. Grandfather Jordan was long gone, but he would have approved of the changes that his granddaughter Georgina had made to the *Countess Aveline*.

'Welcome aboard, Miss Jones. You are Miss Jones, aren't you? No one told me what you would look like,' said a young officer, stepping forward to greet me on the quayside. The ship was moored starboard to the pier. They had been expecting me off the Gatwick flight. I didn't have to go through the tiresome check-in routine that new passengers had to endure. I was crew.

'Well, now you know,' I said. 'And who are you?'

'I'm a deck cadet,' he said nervously. 'No one, really. Everyone else seems to be busy.'

'There's nothing wrong with being a deck cadet,' I said. 'Everyone has to start somewhere.'

'Follow me, please.'

I followed him up the crew gangway, a steward also following with my suitcase and flight bag. This was service. I was used to carrying my own luggage.

'When did you get here?' I asked.

'This morning. Early. We had passengers to disembark and now we have a new crop arriving. They will be coming on board from mid-morning onwards. I'll take you to your cabin first and then send someone to take you to the entertainment director's office. It's a brand-new office.' The young cadet seemed anxious to get rid of me. He was nervous. First tour of duty.

'Lovely,' I said, with faint enthusiasm. My office on the *Georgina* had been a couple of crowded rooms backstage.

Hardly room to swing a computer.

The cabin was low down in the deck hierarchy, but it was an outside stateroom with a decent picture window, sitting area with sofa, writing desk and flat-screen television. The bathroom was a dream, laid out with every toiletry known to women, down to cotton buds and emery boards.

'I hope you will be comfortable,' said the young cadet, still agitated. 'Please phone the housekeeper if there is anything you need.'

'Thank you very much,' I said. 'What did you say your name was?'

He hadn't said. But he had already gone. So had the steward. There was a lot to do with new passengers arriving. At least they had left my suitcase.

As well as being a speedy packer, I could unpack at speed, too. I would be needing an evening dress for the first night, and I shook out my favourite black silk chiffon with the fishtail hem. The show must go on.

There was no point in waiting for someone to escort me to the entertainment director's office. I had to find my own way around this huge ship. I also had to find the crew office to sign on, get my photo taken for a crew card, sign lots of papers and fill in forms about state of health. Current state of health: worn out.

There was the usual pocket map of the decks tucked into all the cruise literature in my cabin. My office was not on it, of course, but ten to one, it would be near the theatre. I headed in that direction. The theatre was called the Acropolis. The world-wandering Aveline Conway had a lot to answer for.

No time to tidy up beyond a quick brush of my unruly hair. Still light brown with a weird blonde streak at the front. Nature had been playing a trick.

After quite a few false starts along opulent corridors and cul-de-sacs, as well as aimless wandering, I finally hit gold and found the theatre. The plush red double doors were locked. A notice said that a rehearsal was in progress. No admittance.

'That doesn't include me, buddy,' I said to no one in particular, pushing open a side door that had been left unlocked.

I was stunned by the size of the auditorium. It was as big as a small West End theatre. Rows and rows of tiered seats stretched out in all directions, and above circled a balcony with even more rows. It must have been three decks high. It was situated somewhere at the front of the ship, the pointy end being at the back of the stage. I could feel the narrowing shape of the ship within the shape of the theatre.

My office was probably at the pointy end.

There was dancing on stage. Girls and young men in rehearsal clothes were going through their routines, taped music blaring. They were good. Good-looking, too. Lots of blonde hair tied back in ballerina knots. And that was only the men.

I sat down in one of the comfortable seats, glad to rest for a moment. My bad ankle was starting to ache. The theatre was air-conditioned; a relief from the heat outside. The music was lulling me into a false sense of relaxation. Any minute I might fall asleep.

'What the hell are you doing here?' said an angry voice. 'No admittance, it says. Can't you read?'

A man was striding up the central aisle from the stage area. He was medium height, but Stewart Granger handsome, wavy black hair brushed off a square-jawed face. His scowling eyes were dark with anger.

'Get out, whoever you are,' he said loudly. 'No one is allowed in here during a rehearsal.'

'Please don't talk to me like that,' I said. 'I've no intention of getting out. I'm looking for the entertainment director's office but sat down to watch the dancing for a moment. They are very good. I'm looking forward to this evening's show.'

I stood up, despite my aching ankle. The flight had made it worse. My rescue remedy was to deny the pain. Tell myself it wasn't happening.

'And who are you?' he asked, thrusting his hands in to his pockets and rocking back on his heels. He was wearing slim white jeans and a white short-sleeved shirt. I could see a glint of gold round his neck. I guessed he was the choreographer.

'I'm Casey Jones, the new entertainment director. I've flown out to replace Tracy Coleman. It was a long flight. I'm tired. So please, I don't want any hassle.'

He started walking round me like I was some animal on exhibition in a zoo. It was unnerving and hardly courteous. I made a quick decision to keep out of this man's way for the entire trip.

'You're the new entertainment director, did you say? Remarkable. I didn't know that we needed one. Replacing Tracy Coleman, you say? The young lady that has gone missing? No doubt she's sunning herself on some beach, stoned out of her tiny mind, surrounded by perspiring local gigolos.'

I liked him even less.

'Now, if you'll excuse me, I have to find my office. There's probably a pile of things awaiting my attention.'

'Allow me to show you to the office.'

He was smiling to himself. From that, I should have been warned, but I was only too glad, at last, to be able to dig into some work. Planning the daily activities on board was a complicated job. It was convenient that the *Aveline* was staying for two days in Acapulco and not leaving until six p.m. tomorrow. It would give me a chance to sort out any problems.

The man in white took me out of the theatre by another side door and along a plush corridor lined with photographs of famous stars and entertainers. Memo to self: take a good look at photos another time. I might be able to use snippets of starry gossip in my introductions.

He opened an unmarked door on the left and walked in. I nearly gasped in amazement. There were three islands of computer desks, each separated by shoulder-height partitions. It was twice the size of my office on the *Georgina*, as well as air-conditioned, light and airy. None of the desks were occupied at the moment; staff probably supervising deck games or quizzes or taking a few moments ashore.

'So this is my desk,' I said. There was a discreet gold name plate with ENTER-TAINMENT DIRECTOR on the wide desk to the left. 'It's very stylish.'

'No,' said the man with some satisfaction. 'That's my desk. I'm Pierre Arbour, the entertainment director aboard the *Aveline*. You are replacing Tracy Coleman, my deputy. Like it or not, you are working for me.'

It was a shock, and I was speechless. I could swear that Head Office said that I was to replace the entertainment director. But I didn't have a tape of the phone call. I hadn't made notes. I was the director on the *Georgina*, the woman in charge of a small but loyal team. The entire entertainment programme was my responsibility and there had been very few hiccups. I could not believe I had been demoted to deputy. Surely there had been a mistake.

'I was given to believe that I was replacing Tracy Coleman, the entertainment director. No one mentioned you or that I was to be your deputy,' I said, trying to keep my voice even and reasonable. 'I am normally in charge. I am the director on the *Georgina*.'

'So I've heard, but she's a far smaller ship. This is a big ship, nearly twice the number of passengers, twice the number of activities to organize, West End calibre shows — altogether a different scenario to your previous experience. I doubt if you could handle this on your own.'

Pierre Arbour said this with such arrogance that I felt like flying straight back to the UK. I was so angry, I could have even flown on my own steam. How dare he downgrade my beautiful *Georgina*, the most elegant ship on the seas.

Hold on, Casey, I said to myself. It's not forever. This is all training. Pierre Arbour was the most repulsive man I had ever met, but I might learn something from him. And I had to think of that annual review. So I swallowed my pride and nodded in agreement. It was an effort.

'OK,' I said. 'So which is my desk? What do you want me to do?'

He seemed surprised at my sudden capitulation. Perhaps he enjoyed a fight. He pointed to the central bank of computers. 'Any one of those. You don't have your own desk. Use what is going. Take a look at the draft for tomorrow's daily programme and check for mistakes.'

Wonderful. How would I know what was right and what was wrong? Did I have a magic wand that would give me instant knowledge of the entire ship and tell me what was supposed to be going on, where and when? I didn't even know where my cabin was. It might be days before I found the Boulevard Café.

'Sure,' I said. 'Leave it to me.'

'Coffee over there,' he said, leaving with a dismissive wave. 'Don't take too long. It has to go down to the printers for distribution this evening.'

This took me back to my early days, when I was the most junior member of the team. The daily programme was a nightmare. It had to tell passengers everything that was going on, from line dancing to art classes, from shows to piano recitals, and from quoits to mini-golf tournaments. And I had to give publicity for all the arrangements for tours so that passengers knew exactly where to assemble and at what time.

I went to the source of all information, a stack of past programmes. This was the middle leg of a long world cruise. It would be making South American ports of call and then some Caribbean islands, including one tiny private island where cruise ships had never called before. That should be interesting.

Despite my tiredness, I had to concentrate. Pierre Arbour was not going to get the better of me. I was going to show him that I could cope and solve those two mysteries. But how? Jet lag was catching up fast. I needed sleep. The computer screen began to blur and my fingers crashed the keys.

So Tracy Coleman had been missing for four days. The ship's last port of call had been San Francisco, an easy place to get lost. Perhaps she had gone on a harbour cruise under the bridge and a dense fog had suddenly come down, as it does. Maybe she had simply had enough of the arrogant Pierre Arbour. I remembered enough of school French to know that arbour was French, meaning shady place or trellis. That ought to give me enough ideas for a suitable alternative name. Woody was too good for him.

When he introduced himself, he rolled

the 'r' of Pierre over his surname so that it sounded like rabrouer, which was French for scold, dress down, snub. Endless possibilities here. This cheered me enormously. Name-slinging should keep me going for the entire cruise.

But I was hoping that I could fly home from somewhere when they found someone permanent to take over the deputy post. They would not want to be paying my full salary for the deputy post any longer than was necessary.

And the missing passenger. Who was he? Were the two events linked? My nose said yes, but all the evidence said no, apparently. What evidence? I'd only been told that they didn't know each other.

First step was to contact the ship's security officer. He was the arm of the law on board, but only the arm. No legs or feet or real authority. He could deal with small infringements of conduct: drunkenness, abusive behaviour, fights and marital disputes. Anything really serious, and a detective would be flown out from the UK and local police from the nearest port would board the ship.

Detective Chief Inspector Bruce Everton from Scotland Yard had been a lifesaver when he flew out to join the *Georgina* following the murder of Dora Belcher, a passenger found with head injuries. He'd given me his personal email address when he left the ship at Lisbon and we'd exchanged a few messages. I'd resisted the temptation to move the friendship up a notch. We were worlds apart and there was that stupid age difference. As if a few grey hairs had any significance. I was the one who was old before her time. I was ageing fast.

★   ★   ★

'Haven't you finished that yet?' Pierre Arbour was back to pour a cup of coffee. He didn't offer me one, only stood and watched me.

'Sure,' I said. 'I can do these things in my sleep. It may be full of mistakes, since I don't know the venues, artists, lecturers or craft teachers. Perhaps you could check it over. Or is it wall-to-wall bingo tomorrow?'

'There are no lectures tomorrow. We have the whole day in port. So you need the excursion details from their office.'

'Thank you for reminding me,' I said.

'Eighteen hours is tomorrow's departure time.'

'Is that why Tracy Coleman went missing? Did you forget to remind her of the departure time? Perhaps she thought, mistakenly, that there was an extra day in port as well. San Francisco is that sort of place. You need two days at least to wander around, get the atmosphere.'

Pierre Arbour did not look pleased. Maybe I was close to the truth. Getting left behind was everyone's nightmare — crew and passengers. I tried never to cut it fine, but there had been times when I'd made an undignified late boarding. Once in Venice, a couple missed the last launch back and hired a water taxi to take them to the ship, fast. The water taxi was stopped by the police for speeding. But at least the ship did not depart without them, and the passengers enjoyed watching the couple's late arrival with a police escort.

19

'I need that programme ready in twenty minutes. I suggest you attend to your work and forget wild assumptions about Tracy's disappearance. I've enough worries without your inefficiency added to them.'

I tried not to grit my teeth; it adds lines. This was going to be one hell of a cruise. 'Are you introducing the show tonight?' I asked, all innocence.

'Of course I am. It's a spectacular, a big show. You only get the minor shows to do or when I'm doing something else. I get to dine at the captain's table quite frequently. You can do it then. Have you brought a decent frock?'

At that moment I was quite ready to jump ship and join Tracy in whatever waitress job she'd found in a fish restaurant in the harbour area. Then I thought of my flat in Worthing which I had worked so hard to buy. And I had to work even harder to pay off the mortgage and the council tax.

'Several. I collect frocks.'

I made it sound faintly rural, all smocking and broderie anglaise without the bonnets. He could think what he liked. He probably had an Armani dinner suit with satin and diamanté lapels.

It was late before I escaped up deck to the Boulevard Café and got myself a cup of green tea. I was into green tea, hoping it would correct any medical problems and ease a sore heart, courtesy of Dr Samuel Mallory. Head Office had pulled a fast one on me and it was not like them. All dealings had always been on the straight and suspicion-free narrow.

The Boulevard Café was half on a sun deck and half under cover. Everything was self-service, and the choice of food was mouth-watering.

Nearby a man sat on his own in the shade, ploughing through a home-made scone, raspberry jam and lashings of cream. A cup of tea was cooling on the table. The well-pressed khaki uniform with gold braiding was familiar. This was the man I was looking for: the security officer.

'Hi. May I join you? You and your cream tea are looking a bit lonely.'

'It's too hot to eat,' he said, his eyes

lighting up a degree. He pushed the plate away. 'More food for the dolphins.'

'They don't throw it overboard these days. Pollution, you know. It has to be bagged and buried.'

'Rather a pity to bag all that cream. Perhaps I ought to eat it.'

'You could try. Conway cream teas are famous all over the world.'

'And you are an expert on cream teas?' It was a mild sort of flirting, pleasant after the earlier encounter with my new boss.

'My daily treat. And you are the security officer? I recognize the uniform.'

'Not many people do. They think I'm a passenger on leave from the Army. I'm Edmund Morgan, Eddie to my friends. And who are you? Not a passenger . . .'

'I'm Casey Jones, the new deputy entertainment director.' I had to force out the extra word with reluctance. Call me humble. 'I'm replacing Tracy Coleman, who seems to have disappeared.'

'Ah, our Tracy, who has done a bunk.'

'What do you know about her disappearance?'

'Not a lot. She went ashore at San

Francisco and never returned. Not a lot I could do once the ship had left the USA. We searched the ship in case she was holed up somewhere, stoned out of her mind. But not a sign.'

'Did she drink a lot, then?'

Edmund Morgan shook his head, crumbs falling off his mouth. 'Not more than anyone else on board. Quite moderately, in fact. She liked a Campari and soda during the day, but ended the evening on orange juice. No, it's just a rumour that she drank. No truth in it. The ship is rife with rumours.'

'But why would someone spread a rumour like that?'

'She wasn't liked. Not by the passengers, I mean; they liked her a lot,' he hastened to add. 'She was popular. It was Pierre who disliked her. They didn't get on. Argued a lot.'

Edmund Morgan chased the last crumbs on his plate, stirred his tea and drank it. I wondered how far I could push him without seeming too pushy. I needed to keep him on my side. So I said nothing.

'Casey, that's an unusual name,' he went on. 'Short for Cassandra, is it?'

'No, it's my initials. K.C. I was christened Katharine Cordelia to compensate for having the surname of Jones. My parents were into compensation.'

'Neat,' he said, standing up and pushing back his chair. 'Work to do. See you around, Casey.'

I quickly stood up. I might never find him again on this enormous ship. 'Can I ask you a small favour? I know it might be out of order, but I'm pretty curious about my predecessor. Any chance of a quick look at her cabin? The answer might be there.'

'Sure, no problem. No one has been in her cabin since she disappeared — I mean, once we took a quick look to make sure she hadn't collapsed in the shower. I can get the key card. Have you got ten minutes?'

I nodded. Pierre Arbour hadn't issued any special instructions for the evening. Perhaps he was giving me some time to settle in. Maybe he had a pleasant streak underneath that arrogant exterior, although

24

one would need the *Timewatch* team digging to find it.

Edmund Morgan was tall. Well over six feet. They often employed ex-Marines as security officers. But he was a stone overweight. All those cream teas, most likely. He obviously didn't work out in the gym. And the gym would have every exercise machine invented, including skipping ropes and big squashy balls.

'Are you ex-Marine?' I asked.

'Yes,' he said. 'Special branch. Intelligence work, very hush hush.'

'How interesting,' I said, hurrying after him. In minutes, I was lost. I had no idea where he was taking me or even which deck we were on. Surely Tracy Coleman had had a decent cabin? I'd always had a good cabin. It had to be home for months. You made it into a home with flowers, mugs, photographs.

'Down here somewhere,' said Edmund, turning along a narrow corridor. 'Don't exactly remember where. We're looking for 516. Ah, here we are.'

He put a key card in to the lock mechanism and pushed open the door.

Then he put the same card into the slot for the light switch. The lights came on. I gasped. I heard his indrawn breath and he stiffened at my side.

'Ye Gods,' he said. 'I didn't know it was like this.'

'I don't think anyone knows.'

2

Acapulco

The room was a disaster zone. Tracy Coleman's cabin had not only been ransacked, it had been done over, trashed, destroyed, annihilated. Every movable item had been smashed, her clothes torn apart, make-up tipped on the floor, her single mattress slashed with a knife. And there had been spray-paint. The word 'SLAG' was scrawled across every bare wall, mirror and picture.

'Ye Gods,' Edmund Morgan repeated. 'What a mess.'

'It wasn't like this when you first checked on her cabin, to see if she was in the shower here?'

'No, it was perfectly normal. A little untidy, but normal for a woman. Sorry, I didn't mean that. No offence taken, I hope. Nothing personal,' he said, stumbling over the words. He was clearly not

27

at ease with women.

'No offence taken,' I said. 'Some of us are tidy and some are not. But this is something else. This is a case of malicious damage. They were either looking for something or acting out in a blind rage. Look at these clothes — some of them have been torn, but a lot of them are cut up with scissors.'

I picked up what was left of an evening dress, a blue tulle thing with sequins. It had been cut into strips, sequins strewing the carpet, twinkling like blue rain.

'I'd better get it cleaned up,' said Edmund, turning to leave.

'No.' I had to stop him. 'No cleaning up, please. There's a lot of evidence here. Could you arrange for the ship's photographers to come and take some photographs for us? No happy, smiling anniversary shots, please. We may need to prove that this is how we found the cabin. We need the photos as evidence.'

'Well, it is evidence, isn't it?' Edmund was lost. This kind of damage was beyond him. 'I mean, we didn't do it.'

'And we have to make sure the

photographers keep quiet about the damage. We don't want passengers starting to panic, thinking there's a manic scissor-hands ripper on board. The cabin has been locked for the four days that Tracy has been missing, hasn't it? Are you sure?'

'Yes, I locked it myself. I came down here with Pierre and we had a look inside to see if she was here. Everything was quite normal. We left everything as it was in case she turned up at a later port. Sometimes people do miss ship-out through no fault of their own, and the port agent makes arrangements to fly them on. If it's their own fault, then of course they have to pay for the flight.'

I shuddered. It was my own nightmare. Missing the ship's departure would be a disaster. I worried about it all the time.

'I know you will have to make a report about this,' I said. 'But it would be better for the time being if it went no further than the captain.' I don't know why I said this. I didn't trust anyone yet. And I certainly didn't trust Pierre. 'What do the crew call Pierre Arbour? Informally downstairs, that is.'

'Oh, we call him Peter-pecker,' Edmund grinned. 'Woodpecker, you know. Not brilliant. We might think of something better.'

'It's funny,' I smiled. 'I thought he might have collected a more suitable nickname. What do they call you?'

'It's not very good. Morgie-Porgie. Because I like cream teas and the odd cake or two. It's all they could think of.'

'When the photographers come, don't let them touch anything or remove anything. Then lock up the cabin and don't let anyone else come near it.'

'Not even the captain?'

'I don't think he'll want to look at it. Steering the ship is a lot more important than one vandalized cabin. I was wondering if, some other time — not now of course, you'll be too busy with your report — if I could have another look at this cabin? A woman's eye, you understand. I might notice something that isn't quite right.'

'Oh, yes. Yes, of course. Any time. I quite understand,' said the security officer, not understanding at all. I was going to get along fine with Edmund Morgan, or Morgie-Porgie.

'And what about the passenger who is missing?'

'That was Henry Fellows. Not exactly missing, as it turned out. Seems he was sleeping it off in someone else's cabin.'

*　　*　　*

I went up on deck to watch the return of the passengers from their tours. Some of them had gone up into the mountains. They were tired from the long trip, longing for a shower and a drink. Sightseeing was tiring and often involved a long coach journey. The best tourist spots were seldom within walking distance of the port.

All the new passengers had arrived and were settling into their cabins and exploring the ship. You could spot them with their little maps or scanning the wall signs. All lost.

'I'd like you to do the quiz tonight,' said Pierre, appearing with a sail-away drink in his hand, although we were not actually sailing away until tomorrow. 'And also the late-night disco. Our DJ, Gary, is feeling under the weather.'

'It must be that fifteen-hour flight from Gatwick,' I said. 'I know the feeling.'

'He hasn't just flown in. He's been on the ship since day one.'

'But I have,' I said pointedly.

'You've got to pull your weight on this ship. No special allowances because you are a woman or jet-lagged.'

'I wasn't asking for anything special. Only an early night because I didn't get much sleep last night.'

'Catch up with naps during the day, that's what I do,' he said. 'And tomorrow, I want you to go ashore and run some errands for me. I shan't have time myself. We're having lunch with some of the other cruise captains in port.'

I had noticed a huge, white American cruise ship anchored out in the harbour. She was too big to moor alongside. She probably had 4,000 passengers on board. Heaven help her crew. Catering must be organized chaos.

'Of course,' I said, smiling. 'Anything to

help out. Just give me a list. I love lists.'

It was true. I do love lists and spend my life making them, using them and then losing them. Current list, already made out:

1. Do everything Pierre Arbour says.
2. Do it willingly.
3. Do it with a smile.
4. Don't do anything extra.
5. Don't tell him anything.

I underlined the last item. I did not trust him further than I could throw him. And that was not far.

For a start, I was not going to tell him that I had seen Tracy Coleman's cabin and the state it was in. I was not going to tell him that the security officer and I were becoming fast friends. I was not going to tell him that I would solve this mystery if I possibly could. Pierre Arbour would wallow in his own sawdust. Timber!

Timber? The word popped in to my mind without thinking. I found it hard to keep the merriment from my eyes. I pretended to tie back my hair with the Conway Blue scarf from my neck.

'That's not the day uniform,' he said. 'The scarf is supposed to be round your neck.'

'I know,' I said. 'I helped to design this uniform. Nice, isn't it?'

Not exactly a lie, but I had been consulted by Head Office. Georgina Conway had circulated the new designs among all top female employees. She was that kind of chairman. Straight navy skirt, crisp white shirt and the Conway Blue scarf. There was no stipulation about where you tied the scarf, as long as you wore it.

'It doesn't matter how you wear the scarf.'

★   ★   ★

Henry Fellows was next on my list. I needed a little more information before I pursued that road. Head Office would not have said he was missing without some reason. I did not want the security officer to think that I was poking my nose into his territory. The dining-room manager always picked up a lot of gossip about passengers. He might know.

It was time to shower and change into my black fishtail evening dress. The creases had dropped out. I was tall enough already and dreaded the prospect of slipping on that stage in front of everyone, so I matched the stunning gown with black kitten heels and silver earrings. No skyscraper heels for me.

A few passengers were already gathering outside the Zanzibar Dining Room, ready for the doors to open for the first sitting. They did not want to get on the manager's black list for being frequently late. He noticed everything. And his memory for names was phenomenal. I often wondered how the staff managed to do it. In a few days, they knew everyone's names.

'Hello,' I said to the manager. 'I'm Casey Jones, deputy entertainment director, replacing Tracy Coleman for a few weeks.'

'How very nice to meet you, Miss Jones,' he said with a slight nod of his head. He was an old-style restaurant manager: black dress coat, polite and formal. 'Will you be eating with us? I can find you a place.'

'That's very kind,' I said. 'But I think for the time being, I'm going to be too busy to eat in the dining room. Maybe I'll take up your offer when I have settled in. It's a beautiful room.'

It was a brilliant design. It took one's breath away. Lots of walled mirrors and chandelier lamps like snowflakes falling from the ceiling. All the chairs were upholstered in pale turquoise brocade and every table had real flowers. Each piece of bone china was in the custom-made Conway design with a wavy blue line round the edge of the dinner plates. Everything sparkled with light.

'Where was the missing passenger sitting?' I added casually.

'Mr Fellows? Over there, on that big table for eight. He was travelling on his own. I thought he might enjoy some company.'

'And he didn't?'

'Quite the reverse. He seemed to be

having a whale of a time. He liked the ladies. They are a very jolly table.'

'And he went missing where?'

'It was San Francisco. I think he got mugged ashore. He always carried a packet of money and waved it around, even though this is a money-free ship. He was a big tipper.'

'Some people like the reassurance of handling real money.'

'I had the feeling it was new money.'

I sensed what he was trying to say. 'Inheritance? A lottery winner?'

He nodded. 'He could have been. All his clothes were brand new. Even his shoes, Rolex, smart cufflinks. He kept admiring his watch. Couldn't take his eyes off it. Now, if you'll excuse me, we are about to open the dining room. Nice to have met you, Miss Jones.'

'And you haven't seen him since?' I was puzzled.

'No, I haven't seen him.'

Edmund Morgan said Henry Fellows had been sleeping it off. It didn't add up.

I thanked the manager and left him to

welcome the diners. It was my opportunity to mingle among the passengers. They wouldn't know who I was, some bird in a posh dress with funny hair and a big smile.

I was beginning to feel sorry for the missing Mr Fellows. It's not easy travelling on one's own, especially if it's a first cruise. Regulars, those who cruise a lot, take it all in their stride, find their way around quickly, make friends, settle into a familiar routine. But to a newcomer, all on their own, it was an alien world, almost weird, however luxurious and comfortable.

The crew would have reported him missing to the San Francisco police, and I wondered if there had been any feedback. Another avenue for me to wander down, by mistake, of course. I could email Head Office and see what they had to say.

I found my second wind in time to run the quiz evening. This was always enjoyable, especially when you had the answers in front of you. The air of competition between the teams was intense, especially when fuelled by alcohol. But the late-night disco was a different matter. I managed to get a prawn sandwich and a coffee at the Boulevard Café which helped to keep me awake.

'No supper?' asked one of the waiters, replenishing the trays with fresh snacks. 'Would you like me to get you some soup?'

'No, thank you. No time to eat.'

'Busy lady.'

'And a tired lady.'

'Just flown in?'

'Yeah. I was in London yesterday.'

The late-night disco was in a small bar on the sun deck, well away from any sleeping accommodation. When at sea, there was little that could be done about the vibration of the powerful engines, but throbbing pop music could be controlled to an extent.

It had been a long time since I had worked a turntable, but I eventually got the hang of it again and no one seemed to mind a few less-than-smooth changeovers. The discs had all been chosen for me, and all I had to do was put them on and make a few introductory remarks. I didn't have a choice. There was no Simply Red or Rick Astley. I was nearly asleep on my feet.

'Is this your favourite music?' asked a voice from behind. I could hardly hear because of the volume of this particular rock group.

'Sorry? Pardon? What did you say?'

'Is this your favourite rock group?'

'What troop?'

'Rock group.'

'I give up. I can't hear a word you're saying.' I turned. It was a pleasantly deep voice, a bit gravelly, and I wanted to see the face that went with it. For a moment I did a double take. I thought that Dr Samuel Mallory had jumped ship and followed me halfway across the world. If only.

There was no red flash on the officer's epaulette, denoting the medical department. It was dark green and gold. The officer was looking at me with some amusement as I quickly searched his uniform for more clues.

'Engineer,' he said. 'Chief Engineer. I

keep the ship going. Nuts and bolts. Grease monkey.'

'Thank goodness we've got proper engineers,' I said. 'I thought someone just wound it up.'

'That's only on Sundays.'

I liked him immediately. Things were looking up. Perhaps I would survive this cruise after all.

3

Acapulco

Chief Engineer Daniel Webster introduced himself over the racket. On second glance, he did not really look like Sam, but there was a fleeting resemblance in the shifting lights of the dim lounge bar. Any tall, dark, crew-cut man in his thirties might look like the doctor. He had the same firm jaw line, same hesitant smile, similar twinkling eyes. Different colour — dark brown, perhaps. I couldn't see in the gloom.

'Why are you doing this?' he asked, nodding towards the turntable.

'I was told to. Orders.'

'Gary, the resident DJ, is over there. He's the one in the loud shirt, dancing his feet off.'

The one in the loud shirt was shaking himself silly in double-quick time to the reggae music. His red hair bounced wildly. He'd have a headache by morning.

'I was told he was under the weather, not well enough to do his job,' I said. Was this the dirty tricks brigade in action already?

'Maybe under the weather this morning after a late-night, but looking bright and breezy this evening,' said Daniel Webster. 'I'll go and have a word with him. He might agree to take over at half-time and let you get some rest. I guess you need a decent sleep after that long flight.'

Another knight in shining armour, minus the white horse. I have several knights dotted around the world, wielding swords at dragons and monsters. I collect them. Things were looking up. Maybe I would survive this social experiment.

'Thank you. I'd appreciate that,' I said, deciding to play a Simply Red track before I retired for what was left of the night. I needed a lullaby of my own.

'Will you be able to find your way to your cabin?'

I couldn't even remember its number. 'Sure,' I said, with a bright confidence I did not feel. I vaguely remembered the deck, the direction and I had my key card. It was a ritual to always check that I had my key card before leaving the cabin.

'Thank you and goodnight, Officer Webster,' I said, on leaving.

'Daniel, please. Goodnight, Miss. Sleep well.'

★   ★   ★

My ears went into shock as I left the disco. They thought I had gone deaf. The quietness, despite the throb of distant engines, was overwhelming. No trouble to find reception. Plenty of signs. Reception was empty of passengers. Only one soul in sight. It was the short-straw staff manning the desk.

A rather wan-looking young woman was on duty, despite the late hour, propping up the counter. She was doing the ship's daily crossword.

'I'm really sorry to bother you,' I began.

'I know,' she said, finding a smile from somewhere. 'You've forgotten your cabin number. Don't worry, everyone does it at first. Have you got your key card?'

I handed it over. She slotted it into the mysterious know-all machine.

'Cabin 333, D deck, Miss Jones,' she said, giving back the card. 'Sleep well.'

'And you. What time do you get off?'

'Six bells,' she grimaced. 'Not long now. Let's hope it's a quiet night.'

'Thank you. Goodnight.'

'Goodnight. D Deck is one above. Take the lift or the stairs.'

I could still manage the stairs, but once in my cabin, I cleaned my face like a zombie and hung up my beautiful dress in a trance. My shoes disappeared into a tangle under the single bed. It had been turned down by the steward.

There was a chocolate on the pillow. 'Sweet dreams', said the wrapper.

My sleep was deep. I fell down my personal precipice into brittle dreams. They say our dreams reflect the anger of the day. I could rarely remember my dreams when I awoke, but I knew that they had not been pleasant. In fact, they had torn me to shreds.

When the sun woke me, for a second I thought I was back in Worthing, on leave, and the day would include a walk along the pier, a stroll through the shallows on the beach and maybe a concert at the pier pavilion. But then I realized we were berthed in Acapulco and I had to run errands for Pierre while he went to a posh lunch on the biggest liner in mid-harbour, swinging its mega thousands of tons on huge anchors.

I went into the entertainment office before breakfast, to show willing. I was ready for any surprises. Pierre was checking his email. He was all geared up in spotless white trousers, white shirt and navy blazer. The Conway tie was missing. Essential, I would have thought, for a prestige luncheon, but I said nothing. Perhaps he was going to add it later.

'I'm sure you'd like a few hours ashore,' he said, as if doing me a favour. 'Perhaps you could pick up a few things for me. In the market there is a local jewellers. Can't remember the name, but it's quite a big, open-fronted shop. I ordered and paid for a ring to be made for me. Special Aztec design. Montezuma dynasty. They said it would be ready on my return visit.'

'Have you got a receipt?' I asked.

'Can't find it,' he said vaguely. 'But they'll remember me.'

'But they won't remember me. Could you give me a note saying I am authorized to collect the ring for you?' I did not intend to be caught out.

'What a suspicious person you are,' he said, reaching for a sheet of Conway-headed stationery. He started to write.

'I wouldn't give it to me,' I said with some spirit. 'No receipt, no ring.'

'And get me some coffee. There's a local brand. Very good. Better than the brew they call coffee on board.'

'OK.' He didn't offer me any money.

'And when you come back, do a check on Debbie. She's doing bingo this morning and deck games this afternoon. See how she's getting on. A bit dodgy.'

'Have I met Debbie?'

'She's our trainee entertainment officer.

Very new to the job, despite training elsewhere. She needs watching all the time. She's always late. I don't think she has ever learned to check her watch or keep her mobile charged.'

'What cabin is she in?'

'Don't know. Somewhere down in the depths. One of the crew cabins. Basic is good enough for her.' He chuckled as if this was funny.

I wondered if she would be an ally or an enemy. If she was getting the sharp end of Pierre's wit, then maybe we would get along fine. I would at least try to establish a friendly partnership. We might even establish mutual support.

It was a relief to go ashore, to shake off the confines of the big ship. The *Countess Aveline* was not yet feeling like home. I knew my way round Acapulco and after shaking off the persistent taxi drivers, I went through the teeming back streets towards the marketplace. It was called a market but it was more of a mix of traders catering to the tourists who wanted to shop somewhere with local colour. The local housewives went to another market for their fresh fruit and vegetables and fresh fish and bloodied meat stalls.

Even if it didn't yet feel like home, at least I was getting used to the new ship's size. The *Countess Aveline* felt like a floating tower block, but she was crisp white and so essentially English. Somehow I could feel the shape of the smaller ship within that she had once been, an integral part of her that one could not deny.

'You come see flea market?' asked a man wearing the badge of an official guide. He was dark, swarthy, with Aztec cheekbones. 'Many bargains. Taxi, then?'

'No, thank you. No taxi,' I said firmly. There was a criminal element in Acapulco that targeted tourists. I had no jewellery on me, no credit card, no camera. I was not going in a taxi to see the famous cliff-divers at La Quebrada, however amazing their skill and daring, leaping down into the pounding surf below the rocks. Leave that to the tours.

'Lana Turner, Errol Flynn, John Wayne, Frank Sinatra. You go see their houses, big houses, very beautiful. Caleta Beach.'

'No, thank you. I have some shopping to do.'

'I take you shopping.'

He was hard to get rid of. I felt sorry for him. The locals had to make money while the cruise ships were in. But eventually he wandered away, looking for a softer touch.

There were over 600 shops strung along the beach and in the teeming inland streets. I knew this market was the showplace for souvenirs, shells, straw hats, leather, ceramics, glassware and jewellery. The place was crowded with wandering tourists and noisy with music and multi-lingual conversations. The jeweller's was an open-fronted shop with glass-topped cases full of silver jewellery, onyx and semi-precious stones, as Pierre had described.

I explained my errand to the shop assistant. The young man looked bewildered and fetched the manager. I explained again.

'Ah, yes, Monsieur Arbour, officer from the ship. We made a silver ring for him. It is ready.' He produced a box with a

flourish and opened the lid. A ruby spat
fire at me. It was big and magnificent. A
man's signet ring. Flashy.

'Very nice,' I said, hoping I wouldn't
get mugged on the way back to the ship.
'Thank you.'

'You pay now?'

'I beg your pardon.'

'Here is the bill. For making ring, for
making ring bigger.'

'Monsieur Arbour has already paid for
the ring, hasn't he?'

'Receipt then, please.'

I could see his point of view. The
jeweller could hardly let a strange woman
walk off with an expensive ring that
hadn't been paid for. Pierre's note saying
I was to collect it meant nothing to them.
I cursed Pierre for not giving me his
receipt. I felt sure he had paid for it. They
were not the kind of traders to do any
work without seeing money up front.

He'd have to do his own arguing. There
might be enough time when he came
back from his free lunch. If he missed our
departure time, guess who would have to
take charge? I was ready. I was capable.

'OK. I'll tell him that the ring is ready but that you would not give it to me. I do understand. You need the receipt.'

I bought the coffee grounds that Pierre wanted and paid for them. Don't call me mean. The packet smelled gorgeous. I bought a packet for myself. Why should I stint myself? I needed the caffeine.

I wandered round the market and bought myself a Panama hat. My hat had gone walkabout. I felt sure I had brought it but somehow it was nowhere around. Lost en route. A hat was essential. Many people forgot about hats in intense heat. The wonder of a Panama hat is that it can be folded or rolled up. Money well spent.

It was time to go back to the ship. I walked, wearing my hat straight on my brow. The local taxi drivers tried again, cruising alongside till they gave up. Energy was returning after sleep. Not enough sleep, but enough to sharpen my wits.

I still could not get over the size of the ship. I could feel echoes of the older ship, could see original woodwork, brass, signs. Grandfather Jordan Conway would have known every inch.

I went straight to the entertainment office. It was deserted. Where was everyone? Pierre (or Timber!) had not yet returned from his free lunch. I left a note on his curved desk about the ring, plus the coffee and the shop receipt. There was no guarantee that I would be refunded. I didn't care. I could afford to give him a packet of coffee grounds, but I'd be warned in the future.

A young woman lurched into the office. She was dishevelled, face flushed, short fair hair like a haystack. But she was wearing the daytime Conway uniform. She fell onto a chair, legs spread out.

'I can't do this,' she groaned. 'I can't do this any more. I've been running around all morning. I can't be in three places all at the same time. Please, whoever you are, I must have some time off.'

'Are you Debbie?' I asked.

'Yes. I'm the trainee. Slave. Dogsbody. Trash.'

'Good heavens, that's a bit strong. Surely it's not as bad as that?'

'It's worse. You don't know it all.'

'Don't worry, Debbie. I'm here now. I'm Casey Jones, the new temporary deputy, replacing Tracy Coleman. Talk to me about it later. But now, go back to your cabin and get some rest. You look as if you need it. Do you have some other duties today?'

'Yes, afternoon quiz, bingo, chocolate buffet.'

'I'll do them all. You go and put your feet up, have a decent meal. Let's meet about five o'clock at the back of the theatre and we'll have a talk. Don't worry, Debbie. We'll work it out.'

The young woman looked at me in amazement as if she had never heard any kind words before.

'I was going to resign. Fly home. Are you for real?'

'I think so,' I grinned.

'Thank you,' she gulped. 'No one has ever said, go and have a rest. I can hardly believe it. I've been working non-stop, ever since I got on at Southampton. It's been a nightmare.'

Quiz, bingo, chocolate buffet. I must be mad. But I knew desperation when I saw it. I gave her a smile and gently pushed her out the door. 'Go, go, girl,' I said. 'Before I change my mind. I'm not into bingo.'

Debbie turned in the doorway, her face pinched. 'Tracy Coleman didn't jump ship,' she said. 'They got rid of her. She knew too much.'

4

At Sea

Pierre Arbour returned from his free lunch in a jovial mood. The American officers had obviously fed and watered their guests well. Americans were a generous and hospitable race.

'So, how is my sleepy little deputy today?' he asked. Now, I am not little. His eyesight needed testing. Five foot eight in bare feet is not little. In high heels I would tower over him. 'No problems, I hope, while I've been away. What a magnificent ship is that *Diamond Line*. She's a floating palace.'

'Everything's gone smoothly,' I said. 'The quiz had low attendance, aimed mainly for the few who stayed on board, but everyone enjoyed it. The bingo was fun. Everyone likes winning money. The chocolate buffet was a gourmet's delight. Even my clothes reek of chocolate. Here's your coffee. It smells gorgeous. And about your ring . . . '

'Ah, yes, my ring. Where is it?' Pierre asked.

'They said they would prefer to see you; to try the ring on, to make sure it's exactly the right size. They wouldn't want such an expensive ring to slip off.'

It's a serious character flaw, these easy half-truths that slip off my tongue as easily as that ring would slip off my finger.

'Ah, yes, of course.' It took ten seconds for the information to register that he had to go and get it himself. It must have been an excellent wine and he had mellowed fractionally. 'Have I got time to go ashore now?'

'You've forty minutes.'

'Tight. I'll take a taxi. Hold the ship back for me, Cassie. Don't sail without me.'

'*Casey*,' I said. I wished I'd told him an incorrect time; one that would have ensured that he missed boarding. Bad, bad thoughts. Lose loyalty bonus points.

★   ★   ★

Thirty minutes later I was hung over the rail, hoping that Peter-pecker would miss the departure time. There was always a hope. All the passengers were safely aboard and the departure formalities and safety checks had been completed. It was a balmy thirty degrees centigrade with a southerly force-three wind.

I would be sorry to see Acapulco fade into the distance. She was so vibrant, so glamorous, the curve of beach a stretch of silvery white. But look behind the glamour and there was poverty and people seeking a desperate means of existence.

If Pierre did not make it back in time, I would be the entertainment director in charge. I was prepared to work hard. Iron those long dresses, girl. You may get a chance to wear them all.

But he made it by the coating of his expensively veneered teeth. A taxi screeched onto the quay and Pierre came sprinting up the gangway, seconds before it was hoisted on board. The captain was making his departure broadcast and the lines were ready to let go. The great ship moved away from the berth, picking up the port anchor, swinging astern before rounding to starboard to head out of the bay.

I was mildly stunned. I had felt positive that he would not make it and I could relax into my new job. But no such luck. The man was with us again, either wearing a huge Aztec ring or not. At least I had made a lot of friends in his absence.

We had two days at sea ahead of us as we cruised towards Nicaragua. I had never been there before. New places were always fascinating. I knew nothing about the country. It sounded exotic. Lots of calypso music on shore.

'Now, let's see what you've been doing while I was absent. Not a lot, by the sound of it. Is the programme ready to be printed? This evening you can do the disco again. I can't stand the noise. And you can introduce the pianist, Rack-whatever his name is. The man is so difficult to please. A Russian immigrant.'

Mentally, I was immediately deciding what to wear, to check the pianist's musical programme, read up on his personal history. And the daily newspaper had to be double-checked. I'd done most of the work on computer before I went shopping for the ring. I'd learned long ago never to leave the worst job of the day to the last.

Romanoff Petrik was very good-looking, according to his publicity photos. One of those lean, Slavic-looking men, intense and hungry. He had a long list of impressive credentials and concert appearances. Tonight he would be playing Grieg and Rachmaninoff. I had an understated silver dress, long and clinging, that seemed a perfect choice for the music.

The grand piano, a Steinway, was in the Cairo Lounge, already in place on a small raised dais. Well-polished wood. I checked that it was in tune. My ear was musically accurate after years of ballet. Passengers could sit in comfortable armchairs, sipping their drinks. It was civilized music appreciation.

'Don't touch, *plis*,' said a heavily accented voice. 'That's my piano.'

I turned slowly, guessing the owner of the voice. He was a hunched giant, intensely staring, black hair tied back in a ponytail, casual black cotton clothes hanging on a thin frame. Didn't he know we had food on board?

'Mr Petrik,' I said. 'Hello, I'm Casey Jones, the deputy entertainment director. I am allowed to check if the piano is in tune. Perhaps you'd like to check as well? It's a beautiful piano.'

He didn't answer. 'I wish to practise,' he said.

'Of course. I'll make sure that you are not interrupted. I'll put a notice on the doors. I shall be introducing your concert. Are there any changes to your programme?'

'No,' he said abruptly. 'Maybe, I don't know. Perhaps, it depends.'

'I'll see you later, then.'

He turned away, towards the piano, and I was dismissed. He was very much the temperamental artist. I left the Russian to practise. As I quietly walked out of the lounge, I heard the first few liquid notes. His touch on the piano was magic. I might enjoy this evening, if I had time to stay.

Since it was such a big ship, it was quite easy to avoid bumping in to Pierre. I was beginning to know his haunts. He liked a Pimm's before lunch in the Boulevard Café, the cocktail of the day in the evening in a different bar, then late-night . . . well, he could be anywhere. It was not that he was an alcoholic, but only that he was rarely seen without a glass in his hand. A sort of stage prop.

I ran into Edmund Morgan. He had that same morose hangdog look as if he had lost something special.

'Would it be convenient if I had a quick look at Tracy Coleman's cabin again?' I asked, before he could change his mind. 'You said I could. You know, the woman's eye? I might be able to spot something.'

'Oh, yes, of course. I'd almost forgotten. Come this way.'

Her cabin, 516, had not been touched. It was in the same state. It still heaved a hefty shock. Who on earth had done this? I stepped warily, in case there was something especially nasty on the floor.

Then I saw it. Among all the debris on her vanity unit was a blue inhaler. Tracy was asthmatic. She would never go anywhere without that emergency inhaler. You could leave the beige one behind — it was only the regular morning or night inhaler — but never the blue one.

'She was taken by force,' I said.

'What do you mean?'

'She left behind her blue inhaler. No asthmatic leaves behind their blue inhaler, wherever they're going. It's a godsend if she has a breathing emergency.'

He was having trouble taking in the meaning of this. I wondered about his background. Was he shell-shocked from Iran or Afghanistan? Security officers were recruited from all the armed forces, but mostly the Marines. They were the stuff that security officers were made of.

'So this means she may have been abducted,' I went on. It was hard work. I was still surfing her ruined cabin. She hadn't taken her sunglasses or her purse. It was difficult to tell from the ripped clothes what she might have been wearing when she disappeared.

'I don't know,' he said vaguely.

'Something must have happened to

her. She hasn't disappeared. And all this damage to her cabin. It's malicious. Some very nasty person has been let loose in here with a knife. Who else might have had a key card?'

'I don't know,' he said again.

'This damage didn't happen by accident. Maybe she was made to watch it happen, to teach her a lesson.' It was a grim thought.

Edmund was nice but useless. I wondered if there was a Mrs Morgan. She must be relieved when he went back to sea. Maybe she sat down, put her feet up and relaxed with a good book and a chilled white wine.

We left Tracy's cabin. There was nothing else we could do here.

* * *

We were soon cruising along the Mexican coastline and in no time would enter the Gulf of Tehuantepec before setting a course across the Gulf. It was cloudy but fine and dry with a brisk north-easterly wind. This is what I loved. The sea, the sailing, the moving towards new places on the globe. I was a reincarnation of Christopher Columbus. I must carry his genes. They say we can, nearly all of us, trace our ancestry back to someone famous.

Dodging the debonair Pierre was a fine art, but I was getting the hang of it. Instead, I bumped into Debbie, our trainee. She looked harassed again. I hadn't managed to have a talk with her yet. The five o'clock talk never took place.

'Is he here?' she asked.

'I don't know. Is there a problem?'

'I'm supposed to be in two places at once.'

'Physical impossibility, of course. Tell me about it.'

'He's told me to do bingo and quoits, both at the same time.'

'Which would you rather do?' I asked.

Debbie looked dubiously at the waves riding by. She did not have reliable sea legs yet. 'The bingo, I suppose. Although, I quite like quoits, out in the open.'

'You do the bingo and I'll do the quoits. Have a quiet bingo and then put your feet up for half an hour if you can. You can't survive rushing around all day.'

She looked so grateful that I felt I might be recommended for a medal of some sort. 'Thank you so much, Casey. I can't work at this pace. Then, this evening . . .'

'Forget about this evening until it arrives.'

It would help to put her mind on hold. She needed a respite. And I needed an ally in this strange arrangement. Pierre did not want me here. Debbie did not want to be here. I was here under pressure. And the *Aveline* was a big ship.

Fortunately, most of the men watched non-stop sport on the huge plasma screen in the pub, the Goose and Gander. It was always full, twenty-four hours a day. And it smelled like a pub. Spilled beer on the tables and floor, despite the heroic efforts of the cleaning staff. I wondered if Georgina Conway knew of the changes to her mother's beautiful ship. I doubt if Aveline Conway ever went into a pub.

So I umpired the quoits game without

offending any of the players. It was so bracing and sunny out on deck, how could anyone complain? I had forgotten my sunscreen, but I kept moving. Quoits could be quite energetic.

It was nearly time to change for the early evening classical concert. Romanoff Petrik was scheduled to perform twice. I presumed that I was introducing both performances, but it had not been made clear.

The Cairo Lounge was full. That was good. I knew I looked a million dollars in my silver gown, hair simply piled up in an array of curls and tendrils with a few combs. Call it casual.

'Ladies and gentlemen,' I said, moving centre stage. 'It is with great pleasure that I introduce Romanoff Petrik with a programme of Rachmaninoff and Grieg music. The programme is his own, and it may change as he plays. He will announce each piece as he plays it. I know you will enjoy every moment. Sit back and relax in to this wonderful music.'

This was pretty good since I did not have much idea what he was playing.

Romanoff Petrik swept on stage. What a transformation. Clothes maketh the man, as Shakespeare said. He was wearing a black velvet suit, the kind of black that envelopes like a glove. A white silk shirt, open at the neck. His hair was tied back with a velvet ribbon. His face was enigmatic.

It was a magical concert. I forgot if I was supposed to be somewhere else. Who cared? The music sent me into another hemisphere, spiralling between planets and stars. When he came off, he was too exhausted to talk. I could see the perspiration dripping from his face. His shirt was soaked. He wanted to get away, but passengers were crowding round him, jostling for a word.

'Thank you, thank you,' he said. 'No CDs. I don't do CDs.'

'This way, this way,' I said, somehow shouldering a path through the clamouring admirers. I got him in to a small side room, where he collapsed in to a chair, cradling his hands. I said nothing, but got him a glass of water. He drank it without a word of thanks.

Then he stood up. 'I go now. I play no more tonight.'

'But you have another performance.'

'Cancel it. I am too tired.'

He nodded abruptly and left the room. I didn't suppose he would recognize me if he saw me again. He lived in his own world.

Supper was a fast Caesar salad in the officer's mess. No time for either dining room sitting. Pierre was making sure I didn't have a spare minute. It was quiz and disco again. I didn't ask why. Perhaps Gary had another hangover.

I began mingling with the passengers arriving for the quiz. It was always so competitive among the teams. The prize for the winning team was a bottle of champagne with house wine for the runners-up. Nothing out of the ordinary. It was the kudos that mattered. By the end of a cruise, it could get really heated.

There was one such team determined to win, three men and two women. They arrived early and woe to any unsuspecting soul sitting at their favourite table. They liked to sit to one side at a low, recessed table in a corner. It was private and quiet. They ordered drinks. I went over to welcome them.

'Hello,' I said. 'That was a good win last night. Did you enjoy the champagne?'

'It was excellent.'

'And we are going to win again tonight,' said one of the women with a smirk.

'We're the best team on the ship,' said the man next to her. I was not sure if he was her husband. They didn't have that together look that some couples have, or perhaps I had paired them incorrectly. 'No one can beat us.'

'Then we are going to have a great evening,' I said. 'The lounge is filling up. We'll start soon.'

'And mind you speak up,' said the second woman. 'You mumbled a bit last night.'

Now, I don't mumble and I wore a body mike which gave me a lot of hand freedom. I knew all the tricks. Passengers often asked me to repeat a question to give them more thinking time.

'I'll speak extra loudly, just for you,' I said.

I did not say that she might be a tiny bit deaf, but the implication was there. My personal ten commandments did not include being rude to rude passengers.

The quiz started. There was a lot of good-humoured laughter and banter, and this evening's crowd weren't taking it too seriously, except the team in the corner. They got quite a bit of barracking from the other competitors.

One round of questions was on Shakespeare and his plays. One wit declared himself to be Shakespeare reincarnated and another said that he had been born in the same year, 1632.

'And you look it, chum.'

'When is Shakespeare's birthday?' The answer was 23 April 1564 and he died on his birthday in 1616, so legend has it. 'And when did he die?' Everyone seemed to know that.

'Benedick's speech in *Much Ado About Nothing* refers to orthography. What is orthography?' I asked. This was a really hard one, unless you had the answers in front of you, as I did. Answer: the mastery of spelling.

'Shakespeare coined the word 'bandit'. What is this word derived from?'

Answer: from the Italian word *bandito*.

We had a quizmaster back in the UK who made up all these questions for cruises. It was a paid hobby. And a nice one, too. I could imagine him sitting in his quiet country garden, surrounded by reference books, scribbling away on a big lined pad.

The team in the corner spent a lot of time huddled together over that one. The woman who asked me to speak up was bent forward and holding her head strangely. Then I noticed that she was wearing a hearing-aid in her right ear, so she was a tiny bit deaf. She was wearing a very beautiful old opal ring.

Then I heard one of the men at the table say, 'Bandit, idiot', quite clearly. There was no reason for him to repeat the question; everyone had heard it.

It took all of six seconds for the penny to drop. That was no hearing-aid. It was some high-tech gadget in her ear. They were in touch with a sixth member of the team, situated elsewhere, perhaps in the library or their cabin, surrounded by books or in touch by phone with someone else.

Or Google. If they had a laptop, they could Google the answer in seconds.

Big problem ahead. Should I challenge them? Declare the quiz null and void? Create a drama, a passenger versus crew scene? Pierre would be on me like a ton of two-by-fours. It was only a hunch. I had no proof. It was really Edmund Morgan's dickie bird. He could talk to them tomorrow.

But I would let them know that I had sussed them out. 'Still having trouble with your hearing-aid?' I asked, leaning towards them so no one else in the lounge could hear. 'Tricky things, hearing-aids. They are so temperamental.'

'We don't know what you mean,' said the second woman.

'I think you do,' I replied.

5

At Sea

The corner team won again. At least they had the grace to look a fraction sheepish as they accepted the bottle of champagne. I made a note of their names, as written on the top of the answer sheet. Mr and Mrs John Fletcher, Mr and Mrs Angus MacDonald and someone who signed himself as T.A. Sullivan. It was enough to go on. I'd worked out that Mrs Fletcher was the woman wearing the hearing-aid contraption.

'Enjoy your ill-gotten gains,' I said merrily, as I handed over the bottle. 'That's a sixteenth-century proverb, as you quiz geniuses probably know. Ill-gotten gains seldom prosper.'

They hurried out of the lounge. I hoped Debbie would get the quiz tomorrow evening when they might have cooled off. I doubted that I could keep up this facade of good humour. It was supposed to be a game, after all.

★ ★ ★

The silver dress was a little over the top for the disco, so I hurried back to 333, D deck and changed into black trousers and a brightly striped silk top. It was warming up outside and the temperature was already in the twenties. Nicaragua was going to be hot and dusty.

'So you have landed the disco again,' said Daniel Webster as I arrived, somewhat short of breath. It was a long way to walk. He was leaning against the bar with a beer in his hand. 'What's the excuse tonight?'

'I don't know,' I said, looking at the play list. At least Gary had selected the CDs to play and piled them up again. 'It's some sort of short straw.'

'Is that another word for discrimination?'

'It could be. I don't like to gossip about my boss.' I started to read the list, hoping there was something easy on the ears that

I would enjoy. Debbie was holding up the bar at the other end of the counter. She was knocking back some sort of coloured vodka. She looked cheesed off.

'Tracy Coleman wasn't that discreet. She made sure that everyone knew what a pain in the rear side Monsieur Pierre Arbour could be. He's two-faced. So charming to all the passengers, officers, company directors, onshore officials, anyone who might further his career. But anyone below his status gets a raw deal.'

'I thought it was just me, because I'm new. And also because I do have the same senior position on the *Countess Georgina*,' I said. 'I'm only here temporarily till they find someone to replace Tracy.'

'Do you? That's interesting. That's not what he said in the officers' mess at supper tonight. He said you were a new recruit and hardly knew what you were doing. Your programme drafts were a mess and you had no idea how to introduce the entertainers. You'd apparently made a haystack of the Russian's concert this evening, and Romanoff cancelled the second performance as a protest.'

I slipped in a CD of Status Quo and turned the volume up. It was mainly so that any explosion of anger couldn't be heard. 'That's completely untrue,' I said, fuming. I was so angry, I could feel my temperature rising and my heart thumping. 'The concert went like a dream. I said all the right things. Romanoff didn't say much afterwards, but then he was completely exhausted. He only said he was too tired to play any more and went to his cabin.'

'He never says much. That's why I was surprised to hear that he had complained. It's not like him at all. He lives only for his music. He wasn't even listening to whatever you said.'

'I made a suitable announcement in the Cairo Lounge later and everyone was most sympathetic. His shirt was soaked. You should have seen him.'

'The man lets his music talk for him.'

That was a surprising comment, almost poetic for a sailor. I was liking the chief engineer even more. He would know how to mend things, how things worked, keep the engines going till I got my orders to fly home.

Edmund Morgan strolled into the disco. It was the last place I expected to see him. His ears were curling, so I turned down the volume.

'We don't do requests,' I said. 'No Elgar or Gershwin in the stack.'

'Ah, what a pity. I fancied a few bars of *Rhapsody in Blue*,' he smiled. It was the nearest Edmund had even got to a joke. 'I got a message on my voicemail that you wanted to see me.'

I nodded. 'It's not desperately important and rather sad, really. But I think I've spotted one of the quiz teams cheating. They've some ear device that they can use to contact and get answers from someone situated elsewhere on the ship.'

'It's called Phone a Friend,' said Daniel, ordering a beer for Edmund. 'Would you like a drink, Casey, while I have the barman's attention?'

'It's probably Bluetooth,' said Edmund, who seemed to know about modern technology. 'Clever stuff. Pretty expensive. It's an open wireless protocol for exchanging data over short distances from fixed or mobile devices, creating personal area networks.'

'Orange juice, please, with ice. Thanks. Bluetooth? I believe I've heard of it. Is there anything we can do about these people? There are six of them. Five at the quiz in the lounge and one more, the Bluetooth fairy, listening somewhere at the other end.'

'The trouble is, if I warn them off, they may not come to the quiz evenings any more. Worse still, they may not return to Conway as passengers again. So the company loses money, rather than merely a few bottles of champagne.' Edmund licked off the rim of foam from his mouth.

This didn't seem fair to me. 'But there's also the other quiz competitors to think about. The genuine winners are not getting a fair chance. The bottle of bubbly might be one of the high points of the cruise to them. Never won anything before, type of memory. I once won an old Scottish pound note, mounted in a frame. I hung it on a wall because I was proud of it.'

Daniel Webster was grinning. 'And what did you do to win that rare note?' he asked.

'I made up a limerick. You know, one of those five-liners. It began *There was an old lady of Sutton, who suddenly sat on a button*. I can't remember any more of it. I think the last line had the word *glutton* or *mutton* in it.'

Daniel sighed. 'Stick to introducing Russians, if I were you.'

'Leave the quiz cheats to me,' said Edmund. 'We'll think of something subtle. It will come in a flash. Maybe we can fix up some interference.'

Both Daniel and Edmund drifted away after finishing their drinks. It had been another long day. I closed the disco at one in the morning. The barman needed his sleep. There were a few murmurs of discontent, but I smiled and said that I didn't have Gary's stamina. He could keep the disco going to any hour, apparently.

Sleep was of the essence. I still hadn't caught up. It would take several more days, and these late-nights were lethal. I wondered what Peter-pecker would have in store for me tomorrow — no, it was today already. No doubt he would think up something diabolical. It was another full day at sea, so he would have plenty of opportunity. No chance of jumping ship.

I was deep in some weird dream about packing when my bedside phone began to ring. At first I ignored it. Then I fumbled with the receiver, not to listen, but to take it off the hook. But half of my brain was functioning, and I heard Edmund Morgan's voice. He sounded shaken.

'Casey, Casey? I'm really sorry to wake you, but something has happened. Something pretty nasty. Can you come? No uniform, just a tracksuit or something. I'll come and fetch you. Five minutes.'

'Why me?'

'I need to have a witness. Preferably female, discreet.'

'Why not one of the nurses?'

'The nurse on night duty can't be spared. She can't leave her patients. It wouldn't be ethical.'

'All right. Five minutes. This had better be good.'

'Good, it isn't.'

It was nearly three in the morning. The witching hour. The ship was quiet and empty, only the night crew on duty. The army of cleaners had not yet started their dawn combat assault on dust and germs.

'Do I have to do this?' It was the small hours, but I tried to look stunning in a dark apricot tracksuit, white trainers and a short, white cardigan. My streaky hair was tied back with a turquoise and apricot bandeaux scarf. I was the fastest dresser in the west and you never knew who you might meet.

It was quite a surprise.

Almost a collision. He was coming round a corner, head down in a file. Officer status, loads of gold braid. He looked as if he had been up all night, too.

'Sorry,' I said automatically. I even say sorry to automatic doors if I make them waver.

'Sorry,' he said in a voice so dark and

deep, it was almost like wading in treacle. I looked at the officer with interest, although there wasn't really time to take in much about him. At a quick reckoning, he was about my height, well built but athletic, crew-cut dark hair and a lot of stubble. I wondered if he was growing a beard. I couldn't see his eyes properly, but I thought I caught a flash of blue. Edmund was hurrying me along the corridor.

'Up late, sir?' asked Edmund.

'Navigational problem. We were heading for Hawaii instead of Nicaragua. All sorted.'

'Goodnight, sir.'

'Goodnight.' The officer strode past, then turned back, looking straight at me. 'Don't often see a vision at this hour of the night.'

'I'm into visions,' I said pertly.

I waited until he was well out of hearing. 'Well, who was that sailor sorely in need of a shave?'

Edmund looked surprised. 'Didn't you know? Of course not, you haven't been to any of the parties. That was the captain.

Captain Luke Wellington. Boots to his friends.'

I tried not to laugh. Everyone got nicknames on board ship. I didn't yet know what they were calling me. One day someone would let it slip. Nutcase would be a good one.

We were in a recognizable corridor, cabin numbers in the low five hundreds. We were going to Tracy Coleman's cabin, 516. Edmund stopped outside, key card in his hand.

'I have to warn you,' he said. 'You won't like this.'

★   ★   ★

The cabin had been partially tidied and cleaned up. I hoped Edmund Morgan had remembered to get photographic evidence. No one would have believed us without some photos. I followed him into the small adjoining bathroom. At first sight it looked the same. Cosmetics everywhere and writing on the walls.

I glanced down. The toilet bowl was full of blood. Some of the splashes were dark and congealing. It was sickening.

'I'm sure it wasn't like this before,' I said, taking a few deep breaths and turning away.

'Perhaps the lid was down. It's not something that would register.'

'Has the doctor seen this?'

'The doctor's coming. Urgent cabin call first. Elderly couple taken ill on A deck.'

'Who reported this?'

'The cabin steward who came in to clean. A young man called Abraham.'

'Why did he leave it till now to report it?'

'There was some misunderstanding.'

I went back in to the cabin and sat down on Tracy's bed. It had been freshly made up. The tumble of shredded sheets had gone. 'There could be a perfectly normal explanation,' I said. 'Tracy could have had a very heavy period. Some young women do. That's why women call it 'the curse'.'

Edmund's face flushed, embarrassed. I looked away. Some men never got used to hearing about a woman's cycle. He had that unmarried, unattached look. A man in his forties who had lost his way. No Mrs Morgan around with a book.

'Er, yes, of course. That could be an explanation.'

'The other explanation is not so straightforward.' It had to be said. I had seen it in my flat-sharing days, long ago when I was a ballet student. Dancers were always beautiful. They had hundreds of admirers. They were also always starving.

'I don't know what you mean.'

'It could be a miscarriage. A miscarriage entails a lot of blood, pain. A woman in pain might be in agony, sitting on a toilet seat.'

I had gone too far. Edmund Morgan looked sick. 'We'll wait for the doctor,' he said. 'We won't make any guesses.'

'If this is the case, then the young woman needs attention. Tracy may be still haemorrhaging. An unattended miscarriage is serious.'

He went pale. 'You mean, she could be on board ship even now, somewhere, bleeding away?'

'She's probably passed out by now. We

have got to find her. And she hasn't got her inhaler. But firstly, we need the doctor to examine the contents of the toilet bowl. Don't let anyone flush it.'

Edmund went even paler. I was beginning to feel sorry for him. He needed fresh air, coffee, a lecture on female endurance. Some men have no idea.

'Let's lock up and leave it to the doctor,' I went on. 'There's nothing we can do except search the ship from bow to stern, every inch. We must find her. Upstairs and downstairs. She could be anywhere, collapsed. In a cupboard, a store room, an unused office. Tracy Coleman has to be found. Can we get help?'

'I'll speak to the chief steward about a search.'

'Good.'

'What about Pierre Arbour? What shall I tell him?'

'Say anything. Scare the daylights out of him. She's a member of his staff.'

'It would be a pleasure,' said Edmund, recovering his colour. 'That man is not exactly my favourite person. He has several times been extremely rude about the role of the security officer.'

'I can imagine. He deserves some straight talking.'

'Straight talking. I can do that. I'm your man.'

I doubted it.

6

San Juan del Sur

I did not expect to be allowed to go ashore at San Juan del Sur. Permission came as a surprise. Tenders were being lowered into the sea. There was no quay long or sturdy enough to accommodate our ship. We were anchored offshore, with the tenders busily ferrying everyone ashore. Two days at sea was enough. Nicaragua was a new port of call for the Conway Blue Line.

Once ashore, I realized why Pierre had so graciously given me time off. There was nothing here. There was nothing to see beyond a wide stretch of flat creamy-yellow sand and a half-built promenade with a few small palm trees waiting to be planted. Behind the fringe of trees was a desolate landscape of high bare hills, rocks and rubble.

A road pitted with potholes and wrecks of cars ran alongside the beach. Shanty huts with bare yards, not a blade of grass or flower, not even a hen or two pecking the dust. Lines of closed bars and cafés showed that this had once been a thriving seaside town. The few bars that did open onto the beach with verandas and umbrellas were not busy. I didn't see a single shop selling anything.

Our passengers were immediately drawn to the local market close to the quay where the tenders tied up. Steel-band music and colourful stalls worked a small magic. But there was a limit to the hats, ceramics, T-shirts, straw bags and carved wooden objects that anyone could buy.

Beyond the market stalls was the real San Juan del Sur. It was so sad. There was one hotel, a two-storied Colonial-style building with well-watered lawns. I could not find a bank or telephone office, nor any school as far as I could see.

'You buy?' said a small entrepreneur. She was clutching some roughly carved wooden ducks. They were hideous. No way could I buy one, however sympathetic I felt. 'One dollar?' she added.

She was about five or six years old, in a ragged pink dress that had once had cheap embroidery along the hem. She was dark-skinned with long, plaited hair and bare feet. One dollar was nothing in today's exchange rate.

'No, thank you,' I said, feeling absolutely mean and wretched.

The beachfront road had not been repaired by their council for years. It was the most dismal walk with nothing to enjoy. The broken kerbs were a hazard. Flood drains pitted the roadside, subsiding into holes.

Guests at the white hotel were not using the beach, but were instead draped round the hotel pool under sunshades and with drinks in hand.

Some passengers had not left the market. One look at the derelict beachfront, and they were queuing up for the next tender back to the ship. There was little to buy, little to drink, little to see. I felt desperately sorry for the inhabitants.

They relied on cruise ships for some income.

I walked along the beach, slapping on the factor 30. The waves were rolling and gentle over a shallow beach. It would be perfect for swimming. But no one was swimming. No one would catch me as the first to disrobe.

Many of the tour buses were returning early because of the impassable roads and abandoned tours. Some of the buses had broken down. Thank goodness I was not a tour escort today. They were having a hard time. It was a quagmire of discontent.

'Can I help?' I asked a harassed escort. She wasn't trained for this. She was a guest lecturer on modern art who had volunteered in a weak moment and was rapidly regretting it.

'Can you help me keep this queue in some sort of order for getting on a tender? Wheelchairs first. It's so hot, everyone wants to get back to the ship.'

'Have you any bottles of water?'

'This hamper is full.'

'I'll dole them out and keep everyone

back in the shade of the stalls while you get the wheelchairs on first. The doctor will not want an epidemic of heatstroke.'

My skin was burning. Thank God for my hat. There were a few red faces and arms. I spotted knees and bald heads that would be painful by the evening.

'One dollar, Missy?' It was the little girl in pink again with her crudely carved ducks. This time I bought two of them. Perhaps two dollars would put flip-flops on her bare feet. She flashed me a big smile and darted away to catch another passenger.

I stayed onshore until every passenger was safely aboard a tender taking them back to the ship. Exhaustion moved in faster than my sunburn. Now I was certain why Pierre had given me the morning off. He was on deck, in the cool, in the shade, already enjoying his second Pimm's of the day, chatting up some lonely lady.

The last tender was crowded and I was the last person on board, sitting on a side seat near the entrance. The spray was cooling and the breeze invigorating. I breathed in the fresh air from the open windows of the tender. It was bliss to go back to air-conditioning, food and running water. Call me a fraud.

That little girl would think she had gone to heaven if she were with me. What could I do with the ducks? No place for them in my bathroom.

★   ★   ★

There was a message on my answer phone from Edmund Morgan, asking me to phone him as soon as I got back.

'You were right,' he said. 'The doctor confirms.'

Confirms what? Edmund didn't say. Was it a heavy period or a miscarriage? I had to know; it was serious. The stewards might not have taken the search seriously.

'Confirms what?'

'A miscarriage of sorts, I think. Of course, Tracy may still have got off at Acapulco and is recuperating in a small hotel.'

'She is still aboard ship. I checked the bathroom when I found her inhaler and,

94

apart from the chaos, it was not the scene of a miscarriage. The miscarriage has happened since. It's recent. She must be hiding out somewhere.'

'Perhaps she went back for her inhaler,' Edmund suggested. 'Sorry, I've got to go. Got to do my daily round. It's expected.'

He did a round? It was archaic. A spontaneous, unexpected appearance would keep the crew on their toes. The passengers barely knew who he was. The khaki uniform confused them.

I had not met the ship's doctor. Dr Samuel Mallory on the *Georgina* was a special friend of mine. He was gorgeous and the toast of all the unattached female passengers. It was a wonder he had any time at all for the medical centre. They besieged him at every corner, every bar, every port of call. Some invented minor ailments just for a few minutes of his bedside manner. I knew the feeling.

But he was a good doctor and put in a lot of extra hours. I'd seen him when he was almost too tired to speak to me. Almost, but not quite. Somehow I helped him recover some sanity.

As usual, the medical centre was many decks below and it took a while to find it. It was the usual spic-and-span area, everything white and pristine. A row of passengers sat in the waiting room, most of them sporting areas of red skin, looking hot and bothered. The receptionist was in a white uniform; a bustling nurse was in white trousers and tunic. She gave the impression of permanent efficiency. She was leaning over an elderly woman, talking to her in a quiet voice.

'Can't you remember the name of the medication you were taking?' she was asking. 'Have you still got the packet?'

The woman shook her head. 'I threw it away, and I've taken the last tablet. I don't know what they are, sort of round and pink.'

'There are hundreds of pink tablets — large ones, tiny ones, round, oblong. We'll have to start from scratch. Please come through to the consulting room.'

The nurse straightened up. She was tall and well built, with a lot of frizzy brown hair. Her face was amiable and almost void of make-up, but her skin could stand it. There was the faintest touch of lipstick. Perhaps the nursing staff was not encouraged to wear make-up. Hygiene, etc.

'Hello, can I help you?' the nurse asked. 'Is it sunburn?'

'No, I'm not a patient.'

'You can see we are busy. Can you come back later?'

'I'm Casey Jones, the temporary deputy entertainment director.' It was a mouthful, and I was sick of saying it. 'I was wondering if I could see the doctor.'

The nurse looked at me blankly as if I were some unknown specimen she had never seen before. 'You haven't done your homework, Miss Jones. I'm the doctor, Dr Judith Skinner. What's this about?'

What an infantile mistake. I should have looked at the crew photos on display outside the library. I had scanned the faces, rushing on my way to somewhere, but only guessed that the female faces might be from the hotel staff or in the purser's office. I should have checked.

'Sorry, my mistake,' I said. I'd only ever met one other female doctor during my years on board ship. It would make a change. No throngs of female admirers at the bar, although perhaps Dr Skinner attracted the widowers who wanted to talk about prostates. 'I'll come back later.'

'Ask the receptionist to make an appointment for you at the end of surgery hours, if she can fit you in. Or ask Helen, she's the head nurse.'

This was efficient and methodical. I never had to make an appointment to see Dr Mallory. It was more a case of fighting one's way through the clusters of divorced women to find him.

'Thank you. I'll do that.' I hoped I sounded meek and grateful. The doctor had to be an ally. I knew from past cruises that it was essential to have a good relationship with the medical staff.

Dr Skinner turned her attention back to the elderly woman. 'Come along, Mrs Smertz. Let's see if we can find out what you've been taking.'

It was then that I noticed she had a stethoscope tucked into her top pocket and a red tab on her shoulder. Casey, you're slipping.

In his office, Pierre was stalking a fly which had managed to evade every known device installed to prevent flies getting onto the ship. It could die of fright.

'Where have you been?' he snapped. 'The tenders have been back ages. I want to organize tonight.'

'There are lots of passengers ill with sunburn,' I said, not explaining how this might involve me. Let him work it out for himself.

'Not your job. Send them to the medical centre. I need you here.'

'I did,' I said. 'It's standing room only down there. Many of them couldn't even find it.'

'I've had a complaint from one of the quiz teams,' he began, obviously relishing the moment. 'A Mrs Lorna Fletcher said you kept leaning over her and she felt intimidated.'

'What do you mean? Leaning over her? I don't believe it. That's ridiculous.'

'It's here, in writing. She even bothered

to write.' He tapped a sheet of Conway stationery sitting on his desk.

They say that attack is the best form of defence and Mrs Fletcher had done exactly that. She didn't scare me. I could use similar tactics.

'Sure, it's because I am tall and scary,' I said, agreeing. 'Fancy poor Mrs Fletcher, who is rather small, feeling scared of me. It must have been awful for her. You'd better get Debbie to do the quiz tonight so that Mrs Fletcher can relax and feel comfortable. Everyone loves our Debbie.'

I slipped in the *everyone loves our Debbie* for his benefit.

I didn't say anything about Bluetooth. It could wait. The right moment would come, if Edmund Morgan didn't lose his nerve.

Pierre looked taken aback that I was not cowed by the written complaint. He swiped at the fly viciously. End of fly.

'I suppose I'll have to find you something else to do. I'm doing the spectacular, of course. Star-billing tonight. Disco, as usual. You could also do the karaoke in the pub bar.'

'Is Gary still ill?' I asked, my voice full of concern for the ailing disc jockey.

'Pretty nasty bug. He's really under the weather. Can you manage the karaoke?'

'Love to,' I said brightly. 'One of my favourites.'

It wasn't my favourite, but it could be fun. It was also scheduled quite late, so for once I'd have time to eat civilized in the Zanzibar Dining Room and meet people. I'd wear something stunning and elegant. Wash the sand out of my hair. And it gave me time to see the doctor.

★   ★   ★

'Sorry I was a bit abrupt with you earlier,' said Dr Skinner as I went into her consulting room. 'I get so frustrated by the number of passengers with sunburn, when they are told morning, noon and night to wear sun protection.'

'Factor 30.'

'Exactly. They always think they are the exception to the rule. Please sit down, Miss Jones. I've ordered some tea. It should be here any minute. I suppose you have come to see me about Tracy Coleman.'

'Thank you. Yes, I was wondering if you could shed any light on the circumstances surrounding her disappearance and the miscarriage in her bathroom.'

The tea arrived on a tray, and Judith Skinner busied herself with pouring tea and passing me a cup. I declined a biscuit. There was a delicious dinner ahead.

'I can't really tell you anything,' she said, adding two spoonfuls of sugar to her tea. 'There's patient confidentiality, even with crew member's records.'

'Did you know Tracy Coleman was pregnant?'

'She never told me.'

'But you did know,' I persisted.

She wasn't saying. She took an exceptionally long time to stir her tea.

'I can't see that this is of any importance.' Dr Skinner was proving a hard nut to crack, but somehow I had to get her cooperation.

'Even so, we have to find her, don't we, and find out? She might be lying somewhere, bleeding to death. A miscarriage can be dangerous if it's not properly attended do.'

'That's true.' Dr Skinner stretched out and put her feet up on a stool. She was wearing Jimmy Choo shoes. Beautifully cut leather court shoes, yellow and red with purple toes. The style was understated, perfect with a little black dress for social occasions but murder if you were on your feet all day.

'Perhaps you could tell me something about Tracy Coleman as a person. It might help.'

Dr Skinner relaxed one degree and began eating a digestive biscuit. 'She was young, pretty in a pert way, vivacious, the life and soul of any party. She put our Pierre in the shade. He didn't like it one bit.'

'He wasn't her boyfriend, then?'

'No way. They hated the sight of each other. They quarrelled all the time. It was like broken glass between them. We tried to keep them separate in case they came to blows.'

'Did Tracy have a boyfriend on the

ship, someone she was really close to?'

'Oh, yes. It was no secret. She had a boyfriend, all right. They were mad about each other. It was that Russian pianist, Romanoff. They spent hours huddled over a piano. Composing music, they said, if that's what you call it these days.'

I stood up and put the cup back on the tray. 'Thank you for the tea. Very welcome. You've been most helpful. I know how busy you are. Doctors are always working, all hours of the day and night.'

She took another biscuit. 'By the way, I got an email today from Dr Samuel Mallory on the *Georgina*. He says he's missing you.' A sudden twinkle came unexpectedly to her eyes. 'I bet he says that to all the female crew. My head nurse, Helen, says she met him once and she has never forgotten it.'

I felt a surge of happiness. It was the best moment of the day. Maybe I'd give him one of the carved wooden ducks.

'I know,' I laughed. 'And he says it to half of the female passengers as well, the younger half.'

I was almost out the door when she spoke again.

'I did some tests on the blood in the loo in Tracy's cabin. It wasn't Tracy's blood. Different blood group. Thought you ought to know.'

I turned carefully. 'Not Tracy's blood? Do we know whose blood it was?'

'No idea. Very common group. I could give you a list of female crew with the same group.'

I didn't want the list, but it could be a start.

7

Costa Rica

The evening had gone well. I wore a silky grey trouser suit that was sophisticated, understated and out of this world. So was the meal, all four courses served with panache. The food had been specially designed. And I met some interesting people at a table for eight. They plied me with wine. I didn't have to buy a single glass.

The karaoke was a laugh. My wits returned and I was the MC supreme. The more everyone laughed, the funnier I got. Some of the turns were really good and some were so bad, it was a wonder the medics were not called. But it was entertainment and that was the point. Don't ask me who won. The voting was hardly first-past-the-post standard.

I went to the disco and cottoned straight onto Gary. He was wearing another loud Hawaiian shirt, girls with coconuts frolicking among the palm trees.

'I'm standing in for you because you are supposed to be ill. What's going on?'

He had that glued stiff, stuck-up hair that had become so trendy and was wearing a touch of mascara. Whoever thought that hedgehog hair looked good? The oddest style for young men. He gulped at his beer, guiltily.

'I'm really sorry, Casey.' He knew my name. 'I've called in sick, really I have. It's an emergency. Pierre wants me to do events that I can't do. I don't want to lose my job, but there is a limit.'

'I don't understand.'

'Deck games. I get vertigo up that high. And refereeing pigeon shooting from the stern. I can't stand the noise of the guns. Now, he wants me to do the seven o'clock morning run round the promenade deck. I'm allergic to getting up early.'

'You might find it invigorating.'

'It would be first-degree cruelty.'

'OK, I get the picture,' I said. 'Now, I am dead tired and need to catch up on my sleep and this noise gives me a creeping headache. I will DJ till half-time, and then you will take over. We'll say nothing to Pierre. How does that strike you?'

'Perfect.' He planted a beery kiss on my cheek. 'You're an angel.'

'Don't push me. I shan't be angelic for long. I'm already shedding my wings. Look, the feathers are flying everywhere.'

He grinned. 'Thanks, Kiddo.'

'I'll even do the morning run for you if you stop calling me Kiddo.'

It was like Pierre to give people events that they could not do. Still, if you joined the entertainment team, you were supposed to be able to do everything. Perhaps one evening I would get the show spectacular and Pierre could wipe off his Max Factor.

★   ★   ★

I had heard so much about Costa Rica and its economic revival. It made me think that the world could learn from them. They had disbanded their entire army. Who needed an army anyway? The

108

money they saved instead went towards education. Schooling for every child, from primary to sixth form. Uniforms for all grades, breakfast and lunch provided. For every child.

Adults did not get benefits to spend on alcohol, junk food and bingo. The money went on the children and their future.

It was a long, narrow quay at Puntarenas, Costa Rica, jutting far out to sea to take big ships. Passengers could walk it or take a little shuttle train. The coaches were parked ashore, lines of them, ready to take passengers on the many varied tours. I had volunteered to do escort duty on a tour to the mangroves. It included a boat trip and I wanted to see those macaws, kingfishers, egrets and herons. Maybe a few crocodiles and butterflies. Perhaps I'd catch sight of a brown osprey flying high.

'You volunteered?' Pierre was nearly speechless.

'They are desperately short of escorts. It shows goodwill from this department. It's only half a day. I can be back on duty all afternoon.'

'All right, then, but make sure you come straight back. On time. No hanging about in the market along the front.'

Our voluble guide, José, told us a lot of things I didn't really want to know. Costa Rica had 120 volcanoes, 6,000 earthquakes a year and 114 different kinds of snakes. And they had one poisonous frog that could kill 100 men. Who was he kidding?

The coach took us through landscape that was dry and parched. We drove over a narrow wooden bridge that was only the width of the coach. It was scary. They were waiting for rain, said José. A fifty-seat boat was waiting to take us along the mangrove river, a muddy twenty-foot wide waterway, the colour of whipped chocolate, with dense forest on either side, branches dipping into the water. Bird song filled the still air, the water cooling the steamy atmosphere.

The riverboat steered a V-shaped channel through the water, washing up the banks, eroding the earth which slid down in miniature rivulets. The excursion boats were ruining the riverbanks. But they brought much-needed money to the people. It was all about surviving.

Sunlight dappled the trees as the guide pointed out birds and basking crocodiles. The crocodiles were difficult to spot, half-submerged in mud and imitating dead branches. Three white ibis were photographic, and a blue heron standing among the mangrove roots was more photo fodder.

I was glad for my hat. The doctor would have more cases of sunburn this evening. When the riverboat returned to the bungalow base, there were cold drinks waiting for us on the veranda. Glasses of mango, pineapple and orange juice. No ice. Passengers were queuing up twice.

I didn't blame them. The mango juice was delicious.

Many of them fell asleep on the drive back to the ship. They missed the scary narrow bridge. Some daredevil photographers asked the driver to stop so they could snap the coach braked halfway across the bridge. I crossed my fingers.

But I'd seen these beautiful birds, flying free, protected in their natural habitat. I didn't care what Pierre had up his well-pressed sleeve. I had done the morning run for Gary, so favour repaid there.

The long string of market stalls along the beach promenade at Puntarenas looked inviting, and as the passengers woke up, they were mentally planning a return to shore after their lunch to spend some money. I hoped they would buy sunhats. It was going to get even hotter.

We'd anchor at Panama City tomorrow evening. How was I going to get Pierre to allow me to go ashore with a tour?

★   ★   ★

There was no time for a crumb of lunch. Pierre had me on a tight schedule. Bingo, deck games, chocolate buffet and the introduction of a repeat port lecture for those who missed it the first time around.

It was teatime before I even got a cup of coffee.

Edmund Morgan cornered me in the Boulevard Café where I was drinking coffee by the gallon. He sat down opposite me and pushed a plate of cakes in my direction. It was kind, but I don't eat cakes. All that fat-inducing cream and icing.

'That blood was not Tracy's.'

'I know. Not her blood group.'

'So someone else has m-miscarried.' He managed the word. Good for Edmund. He was improving. 'Some other young lady is in trouble.'

'*Was* in trouble,' I corrected. 'But she might still need medical help. The doctor should be the first to know.'

'So it still doesn't help us find Tracy Coleman?'

'No, we are back to square one there.'

He began to nibble at one of the cakes. A pink fondant square with a marzipan flower on top. It was chock-full of deadly calories, salt and fat that went straight to his unforgiving waistline.

'I believe Tracy is still on board. She didn't leave the ship at Acapulco, or she would have taken her inhaler. An asthmatic never stirs without it.'

'Unless she was forcibly removed?' said Edmund, with an unusual degree of insight. 'Perhaps she got off today or yesterday. Someone could have smuggled her off.'

I remembered all the wheelchairs. One might have slipped through without being scanned. Getting wheelchairs aboard tenders is always such a complicated procedure, I often wonder if it's worth it. But I suppose it is a stab at freedom for the mobility they used to have.

'Unfortunately, that is a possibility. Did she have any enemies? Rivals? People who hated her?'

'She was popular everywhere. Bubbly and good fun. As I said, the only person who didn't like her was Pierre. She outshone him in the popularity stakes.'

That man again. It was too easy to suspect him of being involved. None of the crew liked him. He didn't like anyone this side of the passenger list. He was the ship's company number-one Mr Nasty. I could buy him a badge.

There was an email blinking on my computer when I got back to the office. It was from the captain. It was brief and to the point.

Dear Miss Jones
Can you spare me five minutes at 1800
hours? On the bridge.
Captain Luke Wellington.

I emailed him back, via reply. *Yes, Sir.*
I could be brief, too. I resisted the
temptation to call him Boots.

★   ★   ★

It was the steepest staircase to climb to
the captain's quarters and the bridge. It
was like a carpeted ladder with wider
treads. I might be able to go up, but I
would never be able to come down,
unless backwards. Although the prospect
of being marooned on the bridge with the
captain for the night was heartening.

Mr Nasty had not been pleased to hear
of my summons by the top man. I had
dropped Peter-pecker as being an insult
to decent trees and birds.

'What on earth can he want to talk to
you for?' he said, as if I was some sort of
frog that had hopped on board.

'It's something to do with carbon

dioxide and saving the world from extinction,' I said. 'I'm sure you've discussed it many times. He wants my ideas.'

'You don't have any ideas.'

If anyone was going to be murdered on this cruise, it was going to be Pierre Arbour. I wondered how I could do it without being found out. He needed to suffer. To know that he was paying for all the cruel remarks he had made in the past, not only to me, but many other hapless recruits, including Debbie. Perhaps I could slip arsenic into his morning coffee? Did they sell it in the ship's shop? Perhaps I could persuade Dr Skinner to slip me a small dose. Arsenic trioxide resembles sugar, is almost tasteless and has been the most classic of poisons since Roman times.

'Don't worry,' I said, flashing a smile. 'I won't drop you in it. Your secrets are safe with me.'

It was a ridiculous remark, but Pierre did not know what to make of it. He immediately poured himself a coffee and drank it.

'Don't take long. There is work to do.'

I knew my way to the bridge. There was a sign at the top of the staircase. SCARY STAIRS — AT YOUR OWN RISK. But Captain Luke Wellington was at the top, holding out his hand to steady me up the last rung. He was smiling.

'Frightening, aren't they? Sorry about that. I've ordered tea, or would you like something stronger?'

'Tea would be perfect. I have to work this evening.'

'I won't keep you long. Come and sit down.'

His quarters next to the bridge were severely masculine. Not a flower in sight. The cabin had two leather three-seater sofas facing a long polished coffee table. The walls were lined with books and nautical pictures. Light filtered through portholes. There was a massive desk in one corner and a massive television in the other. Two inside doors led to his sleeping quarters and perhaps a bathroom. I was never going to find out, alas. He was married to his job.

A stewardess appeared with a tray of

tea. I poured it into two cups. No biscuits and no cake. I handed him a cup of tea. He could put in his own sugar.

Captain Luke Wellington got straight to the point.

'I understand from the shore grapevine that you are quite good at solving mysteries,' he said. 'It was flags and hand signals,' he explained with a smile.

'Guesswork and good luck,' I said, forever modest.

'I want you to find Tracy Coleman,' he said. 'She didn't get off at Acapulco, unless she jumped. Her swipe card was not used. She must still be on board. This ship is like a floating prison. There's no way of getting away unobserved. There are cameras everywhere.'

'A luxurious prison,' I said. 'All mod cons.'

'Hardly luxurious, if you are stuffed into a hold several decks down. She's here, somewhere. I want you to find her. No, I'll put it stronger than that. You must find her.' He hadn't touched his tea. The atmosphere was charged with his firmness of purpose.

'It isn't easy. Pierre Arbour is on my back, not literally, but most of the time. He's probably counting the minutes that I am up here with you. He seems to have an inbuilt aversion to female staff.'

'Have you ever thought it might be insecurity? You are very efficient.'

'And maybe I'm half an inch taller.'

'I'm going to give you special access to all areas of the ship. A signed permit from me allowing you to go anywhere. I don't know, at the moment, what else I can do. I can hardly tell Monsieur Arbour to release you from all duties. It would look suspicious. You know, interdepartmental collusion?'

For a moment, his eyes twinkled. I liked the way they twinkled, shot with stars that were a million years away. I had to hold on to my cup, because my hand weakened. Captain Luke Wellington was ordinary good-looking, but there was something so likeable about him. Good looks are not everything. At first, they are important, stunning, below the belt. But later, it's the person within that matters.

'A permit would be wonderful,' I

managed to say. 'Brilliant.'

'And if there is anything else . . . ?'

'I'll let you know. Is email all right?'

'Yes. Quicker than the phone sometimes. Now, I have to go. Steer the ship somewhere. Where are we going? Ah, Fuerte Amador. Bad weather ahead, apparently, force six to seven. Hold on to your hat.'

'And so do I, have to be somewhere, that is. Thank you for the tea, sir.'

'Call me Luke.

'Call me Casey.'

I walked on air.

He showed me to a private lift. It took me all the way down to the Zanzibar Dining Room. At least I knew where I was now. I was back in the entertainment office in less time than it takes to tell.

★   ★   ★

When I got back, Pierre was doubled up over his desk, his face white.

'I'm ill, Casey,' he groaned. 'I've got the runs. Something I ate. Seafood last night, maybe. I had rather a lot. You'll have to do the spectacular this evening. Don't mess it up. I'm relying on you.'

'You need the doctor,' I said quickly. He really did look quite ill. 'Or a nurse. Let's get you back to your cabin.'

'But the spectacular?' he groaned again.

'Don't worry, I can do it. You go to bed and sweat it out. It's only another show.'

'Do what you like,' he croaked. 'I'll sort out your mistakes when I'm better.'

Charming.

'You take care,' I said, slipping instantly in to motherly-nurse mode. My mother would have given him a double dose of Syrup of Figs. 'Drink lots and lots of liquid. You mustn't get dehydrated.'

His answer was an incoherent mumble. The melodious tone of the voice beautiful was on hold.

*　*　*

Yes, it was only another show. But I knew how to present it, twice in one evening. I wore my beautiful layered Versace dress, one of my top favourites. It was several layers of voile, from dark rose to the palest sweet-pea pink. The overlapping layers flowed round my ankles like foam. I'd been saving it for an occasion, and this was just such an occasion.

Everyone had had a lovely day in Costa Rica. I loved the country; it had captured my heart. Captain Wellington had faith in me and was giving me a permit to move anywhere round the ship.

The audience in the Acropolis Theatre was glad to see a different face, with bare arms and shoulders. Pierre never bared his shoulders, except maybe round the pool. Though, to be honest, I had never seen him round the pool. Perhaps he had moles or warts.

It was a *spectacular* spectacular. A West End singing star, a talent-winning dance troupe, acrobats from Russia on the way up. Pop stars on the way down. I gave them all the biggest build-up. So easy to introduce artists that were brilliant. Mediocre shows were the devil.

Male passengers were pleased to see lots of female flesh and a smile that could sink a thousand ships. If Helen of Troy could do it, so could I. Cheers and wolf whistles followed my stage exit. Everyone was in a good mood, ready to enjoy themselves. Several of the artists thanked me for my complimentary build-up.

'We'd better be good after that introduction.'

It was a truly memorable evening. People stood and clapped and it was not because of me. I was only a floating female figure in pink voile who wafted on and off stage, saying all the right things. It was the memory and the future fused together. They wanted the good life to continue.

I was in the Boulevard Café boosting my energy levels with a quick salmon sandwich and a coffee before the end of the second show, when Edmund Morgan hurriedly approached my table.

'Sorry, Casey,' he said. 'A disaster. Something dreadful has happened.'

'Oh dear,' I said, halfway through a mouthful. 'Am I involved?'

'Not really. Someone poured cleaning spirit into the cabin of Pierre Arbour while he was asleep. Toxic fumes, etc.

He's in intensive care.'

I was involved, deeply. But I had an alibi. Several hundred people had seen me on stage, twice, and talking and waiting backstage during the show. They couldn't blame it on me.

'Is he going to be all right?'

'He'll survive. Luckily, Helen, the nurse from the medical centre, had called in and was able to move him to a private room.'

'This is really awful, but can I talk to you later? We are all madly busy, being one short.'

'Sure. I'll catch up with you later.'

It was so peaceful without Pierre, but I was the tiniest bit sorry about the cleaning fluid. Was it a message or a warning from someone? We were busy, but I enjoyed rushing round at my own pace. Gary and Debbie had found renewed enthusiasm now that the yoke had been lifted and took on the extra work without a grumble. They knew I was doing more than my fair share.

'Thank you, Casey, for giving me an easier time,' Debbie said. She was on her way to the quiz. At least she could sit at the table and read the questions. 'Really appreciate it.'

'I looked at the schedules, and Pierre has been giving you a load of work since the ship left Southampton, while he did hardly anything. But all that is going to change now if he is out of action.'

I was trying to make sure that Debbie did not do too much. She was still pale and seemed to sit down a lot. Once I saw her leaning against a wall, catching her breath. It was not natural in a young woman. She was in her mid-twenties. Then the penny dropped. With a clang.

She ought to see Dr Skinner. Now.

8

At Sea and Fuerte Amador

'Debbie,' I said, taking her aside to a quiet spot. 'I'm sorry we didn't make that time at the theatre.' She wouldn't look at me, instead staring at the carpet. 'You can tell me to clear off and mind my own business, but why don't you go and see Dr Skinner now? You seem very much under the weather, despite the temperature outside, and I'm really concerned about you.'

Her reaction was unexpected. She staggered to sit down on a nearby chair and burst in to tears. She sat, clutching her stomach, her face an unhealthy pallor.

'Are you in pain?'

She nodded like a rag doll.

'Are you bleeding? You have to tell me. I can help you.'

'A l-lot.'

'Is it what I think? Come on, we are both grown-ups.'

She nodded, still sobbing.

'You must go and see the doctor now. I insist. No arguing, Debbie, please. I'll cover for you. I'll have time to do the quiz. It can start a bit later.'

Debbie did not need to be told twice. She looked relieved that her condition had been recognized by a sympathetic woman. It was not the first miscarriage I had seen. My years at ballet school had been educational in more ways than learning how to dance *sur les pointes*.

'I feel awful,' she said, wiping her tears with a tissue. 'So low and so weak. Please don't think it was my fault, that I did anything. I wanted that baby. But now I think something went wrong. I was afraid to go to the doctor in case she thought I had done something to myself and I got sent home. I need this job. I love it and I want to make it a career. I want to be successful like you, Casey.'

Successful like me? Was I successful? Tell me about it when you've got a few hours or a week.

'I won't say a word to Head Office if you go straight to the doctor now. I'll also speak to Dr Skinner and ask her not to report your condition. You should be back on your feet in a couple of days, perhaps even sooner, feeling much better. Does the father know about the baby?'

Debbie looked wistful. 'He doesn't know. He wouldn't want to know.'

Married? It was not my place to probe.

★   ★   ★

After the shows, I made a lightning-quick change into black trousers and silky top for the quiz. I wondered how the cheating table would take my reappearance. Edmund had not spoken to them. Maybe they would realize that they had been rumbled.

The corner group was one member short; the tiny woman with the Bluetooth aid in her ear had not arrived. Perhaps she was ashamed. It could happen.

We were halfway through the quiz. 'What was the name of the dance group which won the *Best of Britain* talent show in May 2009?' I asked.

Edmund appeared in the doorway of the lounge. He looked worse than ever, hair falling over his eyes, bewildered, disorientated, like little boy lost. He came over to my table. The man was a mess.

'Can I speak to you?' he asked in a low voice.

'Sure. We are just about to take five. Take five, everyone! Time to renew your drinks. What is it, Edmund? You look worried.'

'One of the passengers, a woman, is dead. I think she's committed suicide in her cabin,' he gulped. 'I don't know what to do.'

'How dreadful. That's really bad news. Call Dr Skinner first, captain second, purser third to inform next of kin. Get going, Edmund. Was she travelling with anyone?'

'I don't know.'

'Is it a double cabin?'

'I didn't notice.'

He was one hopeless security officer. I could run rings round him. 'Come along, let's find out,' I said, leaving the quiz players to gather at the bar for refills. 'Start phoning as we walk. Are you sure the woman is dead?'

Edmund nodded. 'She looks dead. She's been dead a while, I think. Not exactly cold or stiff, but quite dead.'

What did quite dead mean? It was not a medical term that I was familiar with. However, I would see for myself very soon.

It was cabin 102 on A deck. An inside double cabin, spacious but no view. It was halfway between a standard and a stateroom. There were a lot of extras. A crew member was standing outside, obviously to stop any steward from going in. This passenger wouldn't be needing any clean towels. Edmund opened the door.

'Are you sure you want to go in?'

'Yes,' I said firmly. 'But remember, don't touch anything.'

The cabin was empty, both single beds turned down, chocolates on pillows. Sweet dreams, etc. Long dreams this time.

The woman had hanged herself with

the cord from her complimentary bath-robe. The shower rail had taken her weight. She was built like a bird. Her stocking toes barely touched the edge of the bath. There was a glimpse of crimson varnish on her toenails. I knew immediately who it was.

It was the missing woman from the quiz team, the one with the Bluetooth in her ear. It was a shock to see her hanging like this. Mrs Lorna Fletcher. For a moment, I felt responsible. But I had not said anything officially. No one had accused her of cheating.

There must be some other reason for this desperate act. No one kills themselves over a crooked quiz game. You might go into hiding, wear sack cloth and ashes, give up chocolate for Lent, but never hang yourself.

Her face was not a pretty sight. Constriction of the throat does horrid things to the tissue of the face, the eyeballs and the mouth. Her face was congested with a blue tinge; the eyes were bulging. There was froth and blood staining around the nose and mouth, her tongue protruding.

She had been wearing semi-formal for the first dinner sitting. A long, black skirt with a white pleated blouse. Her necklace had broken and the beads were strewn all over the bathroom floor. Also on the floor was a pair of silver sandals, kicked off.

'Do you know who she is?' I asked.

'Not yet. Can't get hold of the purser.'

'This is the woman who was cheating at the quiz. Her name is Mrs Lorna Fletcher. Mr Fletcher is doing the quiz. Perhaps we ought to send for him.'

Edmund was on his mobile again. It was his safety net. His barrier against the world. He'd phone anyone, rather than talk face to face.

'Don't you think it would be polite and more official if you fetched Mr Fletcher from the lounge yourself? There's nothing for you to do here. You could break the news gently to him, away from his friends. It would be better than sending an officer,' I said.

'I suppose so,' said Edmund. He flashed me a smile. 'Thank you, Casey. I hadn't thought of that.'

It also gave me a few moments alone with the dead woman. Reducing or cutting off the oxygen supply to the lungs is known as asphyxia, and that seemed to be the cause of Mrs Fletcher's death. It's not an easy death. It can take as long as five minutes. The natural reaction is to struggle for breath. There's the slowing down of the heart. But sometimes the heart stops before the asphyxiation is complete.

The horizontal mark of the ligature was visible under her neck, but it sloped upwards towards the shower rail. It had only been a short drop, but then it has been proved that simply jerking the head back can fracture or dislocate the vertebrae near the brain and cause instantaneous death.

Those broken beads said something, but I did not know what. I looked at her nails. They were broken. Had she struggled, or did she bite her nails? The kicked-off silver slippers . . . on purpose or in desperation? I was not yet convinced that this was a suicide. There was no note anywhere. Suicides usually leave a note.

My acute hearing picked up footsteps coming along the corridor, and I stood back from the corpse. She was still slightly swinging with the ship's movement. Mr Fletcher was in for a shock.

He nearly passed out. We had to get him to a chair, pour him a glass of water. Fortunately, Dr Skinner arrived at the same moment, and she was able to administer to both the living and the dead. Minutes later, Captain Luke Wellington arrived on the scene and was a stabilizing factor. He knew exactly what to do. He didn't run a big ship for nothing. *Countess Aveline* was a big ocean-going liner and people died. We were like a big village. Death happened.

The captain caught sight of me in the background and nodded recognition but no more. It was not appropriate. He took in the scene wordlessly, not missing anything. Then he looked at me and his eyes had an urgent message. He seemed to be telling me to look into this death, too.

I suddenly thought of Henry Fellows. Had anyone seen him around? Edmund had said he was all right and had only been sleeping off a heavy night. I had almost forgotten all about him in my focus on Tracy Coleman and keeping Pierre off my back.

The captain spoke to Dr Skinner in a low voice and then went to talk to the distraught Mr Fletcher.

'I don't understand,' John Fletcher said. 'Lorna had no reason to take her own life. We were all joking and laughing at dinner and looking forward to the quiz. We're the star table, you know. We nearly always win. This is just not like her. She's a very confident, capable person, not upset or nervy at all.'

'But she wasn't at the quiz tonight?'

'No, no, she said she had a headache. Very unlike Lorna. She's not a headachy person. Never had one in her life before, as far as I can remember. I can't believe this. It's all unreal.'

Dr Skinner had closed the bathroom door so that she could make her first examination of the body. A few moments later, she returned and sat beside Mr Fletcher. Her face did not betray any emotion, but her voice had softened with sympathy.

'Mr Fletcher. I'm really sorry. This is a big shock for you.'

'I can't believe it.'

'I will need to make a further examination, Mr Fletcher. Although it does look as though it's an act of suicide, it may be that she had an aneurysm and the pain was too much to bear.'

'An aneurysm? That's a clot or something, isn't it?'

'It's the weakening of the wall of a blood vessel, usually in the brain, abdomen or chest. The rupture of the aneurysm, that is the breaking of the weakened wall, can be fatal and cause death. I should need to investigate.'

'Do what you have to do,' he said gruffly. 'We have to find out why she did this needless thing.'

'Would you like me to inform anyone at home?'

'No, we don't have any children. There's no one.'

'Then, when you feel more like it — not now, of course — we need to discuss any necessary arrangements.'

For a moment, he looked bewildered. 'Arrangements?'

'There are several options,' Captain Wellington said swiftly. 'But there's no need to talk about them now. I suggest that the company of friends might help and a cup of tea, perhaps a walk round the deck.'

'I'll go back to the quiz,' I said. 'I'll ask Mr MacDonald and Mr Sullivan to come and keep you company. Would that be all right?'

'Not Ted Sullivan,' said John Fletcher, with a sudden burst of anger. 'Can't bear the sight of the man. Just the Mac-Donalds, Angus and Fiona.'

* * *

It was not easy to go back to the quiz after seeing Lorna Fletcher's body in the bathroom. I had to stand outside the lounge and take a couple of deep breaths. But the show must go on, the cruise must go on, life must go on. I put a small smile on my face and went into the lounge.

The corner table was empty, and the atmosphere was so heavy, you could have strung lights on it. The grapevine had started its tortuous means of finding out what had happened.

'Are you all right?'

'Something wrong, Miss Jones?' someone asked.

I couldn't pretend it was nothing. My face probably gave away my feelings. I had been trained as a dancer, not an actress.

'An accident,' I said. 'I'm afraid that's all I can tell you. Now, where were we? TV dance troupe. What's next? Ah, yes. Questions on ancient Egypt.'

There was a general lightening of mood and a universal groan. 'Not the pyramids again? How long did they take to build? The Great Pyramid of Cheops, one of the Seven Wonders of the World. Same old questions.'

'Some new questions, I promise you,' I said, hoping that I was right. 'When was the great period of pyramid-building?'

Dates were not the tops in their agendas, so I knew there would be some wild and woolly answers.

'Which of the pyramids was the perfect place to celebrate the birth of the millennium?'

Blank looks. Now this floored them. I thought it would. Answer: the Great Pyramid of Giza.

★   ★   ★

We were on a north-easterly course towards the entrance of the Panama Canal, and towards our designated anchor position. There was quite a strong wind outside and it was getting stronger. It seemed we were in for a rough day at Fuerte Amador, the port for Panama City. Captain Wellington had said the weather was worsening.

Panama City was always a joy to visit. I'd been there before and it was a great place, so varied as the result of so many different civilizations making their home there. Would you expect to see castles and medieval ramparts in somewhere that sounded as new and as glamorous as Panama City? Their presence always came as a surprise.

I was trying to hold the quiz together despite the rising sound of the wind. Several women looked anxiously out the windows, but there was nothing to see.

But something was happening outside the lounge, some sort of commotion. John Fletcher came in, almost staggering. His face was red and he was dishevelled, not like his usual self.

'Where's that bastard?' he was shouting. 'Where's that Ted Sullivan? I'm going to kill him.'

9

Panama City

The strong winds could not be helping Pierre's delicate condition, whatever it was. He sent a handwritten note to the office to say that he was taking a few days' sick leave. It was not addressed to me. I didn't exist. The dame with no name.

I tried to find out more about the cleaning fluid, but Pierre had returned to his cabin and was not talking to anyone.

After a busy day, I gave myself permission to go ashore as an escort on the evening tour to Panama City. I'd seen it myself and loved the city, but I wanted to watch people's reactions and their amazement as they discovered the three faces of the city.

Pierre's illness was still undetermined. Dr Skinner had not been called to his cabin. Apparently, this was not unusual.

'I'm afraid Monsieur Arbour has a

variety of ailments to call upon,' she told me over a quick cup of coffee in the Boulevard Café. Her eyes were twinkling again. 'He's got the three-day work syndrome.'

'The three-day work syndrome? What's that?'

'Three days of work and then he has to take the rest of the week off. He should have my job.'

I had to laugh. Trawling through the paperwork and computer files had been an eye-opener. Pierre put himself down for very few events, apart from the nightly stage show. Occasionally, he did an afternoon interview if it involved talking to a celebrity on stage. Unless he regarded the daily circulating of the bars as work. In which case, he could probably clock up overtime.

Maybe he had his own bottle of cleaning fluid.

But this evening, it was the excursions team working overtime. They had to reschedule all the trips because the *Aveline* had lost its berth in the inner harbour. The weather had delayed our arrival, and a huge cargo ship had taken our slot. It was not long enough to take two vessels, so we were anchored outside and the tenders were lowered to take passengers on a rough ten-minute trip to the quayside.

The weather was deteriorating. Although it was a warm 29 degrees, the north-easterly wind was a ferocious force six to seven. For a while, I thought the whole programme might be cancelled. Stepping onto a rocking tender could be tricky. Sensible shoes were the order of the day. It still horrified me when I saw high heels or flip-flops worn for the roughest territory.

'Don't you have any trainers?' I asked one woman, already staggering on four-inch stilettos. 'It's a bit rough out there.'

'But these match my outfit.'

'I don't think the fish will notice.' Oh dear, broken one of my ten commandments. 'Just a joke,' I added comfortingly. 'The crew will help you.'

But she did go and change her whole outfit. She saw sense.

The tenders were being buffeted by the

strong swell, and it looked like quite a few passengers were beginning to wish they had stayed on board and watched a film. A few opted out. I wore a light blue trouser suit so that I could be easily spotted as it grew dark and tied my hair back with a Conway silk scarf.

Ted Sullivan was in my group. John Fletcher had obviously not bumped him off yet. He was a swarthy individual with a mass of unruly dark hair and a five-o'clock designer shadow to match. He might have been in his late thirties or a well-preserved forty. His neck was slung with an array of straps of an expensive camera and video equipment. There was nothing aggressive about him.

He was accompanied by a vivacious silvery-blonde woman, apparently called Gina, who could have been any age from forty to sixty. She'd had her fair share of Botox. 'I hope we get plenty of time for serious shopping,' she trilled, patting a large gold shoulder bag. Her earrings were the size of saucers.

My coach tour wasn't going to do any

shopping, apart from Adelia's souvenir shop, a compulsory comfort stop.

I was glad to get out of the tender and onto dry land. I had a good pair of sea legs, but not in a lurching bucket. It had been quite alarming.

'That was a bit rough,' said Ted Sullivan, grinning.

'I like a bit of rough,' said Gina.

I herded my group onto minibus twenty-one, counted heads, then we were driven downtown. It was a depressing sight: street after street of empty, tumbledown buildings, graffiti on the walls. The result of an earlier economic depression. The first city of Panama was completely destroyed by a pirate called Henry Morgan in 1671, when he set fire to the wooden township. It looked as if the pirates had made a second visit. Only one piece of original wall remained.

Next we reached the French Quarter: the white, stone colonial houses and embassies, the Margot Fonteyn theatre with its beautiful Roberto Lewis ceiling and gold and white balconies. It was a fairy-tale palace. We walked the Esteban

Bridge, over the top of dungeons, gawped at the palatial social club for rich people and spotted the presidential police. A different world.

The contrast was difficult to absorb. But then Panama City was difficult to understand. It was a city cloaked in magic.

The colourful *diablo rojo* buses were a great hit, though confusing for the tourists who tried to use them. The drivers personalized them to commemorate great artists or singers or performers. But at first their routes remained a mystery.

All this grandeur grew during the construction of the Panama Canal, and the huge resulting influx of workers, the French engineers and their families.

'Lovely, lovely,' said Gina, the shop-aholic. She bought armfuls at the souvenir shop, including a black lace shawl which she immediately draped over herself with stunning effect.

Our driver and guide, Pepe, took us through the city, filled with wall-to-wall white skyscrapers and eighty international banks. Eight-0. Even Donald Trump had built another Trump Tower here. It spelled money on every floor.

Lastly, we drove to the outskirts of the new city towards the old city, Old Panama or *Casco Viejo*, where the ruined cathedral dated back centuries. It was once a vast building in the shape of a cross. So many races, so many cultures, were all crowded into these acres of rough ground. We were treading on history. We saw what was left of the Bishop's House, the old fort, the monastery and a tall bell tower that was open to the elements, but you could see a set of steep wooden spiral steps going right to the top.

I tried to imagine the medieval workmen's task of building those steps, without modern scaffolding and machinery. The same pirates destroyed all this in 1519. These marauding pirates had a lot to answer for, but somehow the spirit of Panama survived.

It was beyond dusk by now and only the ruins were floodlit. There were dark areas of gloom to walk through with shifting shadows and trees. I hoped no one would fall on the rough ground. It was every escort's nightmare, an injured passenger to get back to the ship, or worse, left behind at a foreign hospital. I wished I had brought a strong torch.

In spite of the gloom and potential danger, the atmosphere had a certain magic. It would have been the perfect place to stage a ballet. The moonlight was ethereal. Dancers could flit from the trees like moths in flimsy gossamer dresses. My mind was drifting back to my heady dancing days. Before I fell and my career came to a painful end. I could have danced here.

'I can't see a thing.'

'Where are we? Ye Gods, it's as black as night.'

'It is night.'

'This way, please. Follow me and Pepe. Be careful of the loose stones,' I said. 'Look where you are walking.'

'Have we got time to go shopping now?' It was Gina's voice. I caught a glimpse of her silvery hair in the moonlight. 'I've had enough of ruins, all these great lumps of old stone. They don't mean a thing today.'

'I don't think any of the big shops are open now,' I replied.

'I thought this was going to be a late-night shopping tour.'

It was time to return to the ship. The *Aveline* would spend the night at anchor before traversing the Panama Canal tomorrow. But we had to be back at the quayside by ten forty-five p.m. to pick up a tender.

I took a head count, although it was not really necessary with a minibus. I knew where everyone was sitting. Four on the back seat, three couples to the left and three single seats to the right. There should be fourteen, including me, and I was sitting on a fold-down seat next to the driver.

Except that there weren't. There were only thirteen.

'Ted Sullivan is missing,' I said swiftly.

'But he was with me,' said Gina. 'All the time.'

'Did he go off somewhere to take an extra photo? Did he say where he was going?'

149

'No, no. He'd given up. His camera had jammed.'

Maybe Ted Sullivan had slipped behind a dark bush. It could happen. It had happened before. People got caught short and there were never enough loos in the right places. There were always queues.

'We'll wait a few minutes. Perhaps he'll realize that we've all come back to the bus.'

'We could go and look for him,' two of the men offered.

'No, no, but thank you for the offer. It's better if we all stay together. I don't want to lose you two as well.'

I made a note of the time. All tour escorts have to fill in a report of every incident. We waited five minutes and then I sent Pepe to look for Mr Sullivan. He fished out a cosh-sized torch from the boot, even though he knew every inch of the ground. He was anxious to find Mr Sullivan. It would show on his record if he was late back.

'Are we going to miss the ship?' Gina wailed.

'No way,' I said. 'She's spending the

night at anchor outside the harbour. And the last tender will wait for us. That's the blessing of our swipe cards. It will show up that the fourteen of us on bus twenty-one have not returned.'

'They'll probably think we've got a flat, or broken down.'

'It's getting cold,' said another woman with a shiver.

It was indeed. Once the sun had gone, the temperature dropped rapidly. I was cold, too. My summer trouser suit was no protection against the night air. My toes were like ice, even in trainers. I needed a fleece and some socks. I took the scarf off my hair and tied it round my neck. It offered some warmth. I should have offered it to the woman who said she was cold, but it wasn't in my ten commandments. Plus, she had a husband to keep her warm.

Pepe was returning across the car park, propping someone up. It was Ted Sullivan. But he was staggering and stumbling and hanging on to Pepe's arm for help. I got out of the bus and ran to help.

'What's happened to him?'

'I found him on the ground, groaning, almost unconscious. But he seems to be recovering. We'd better get him to the city hospital.'

'Which is the nearest, the city hospital or the ship?'

'The ship.'

'Then we'll go to the ship. We've all the medical facilities we need there. I'll phone ahead for a medic to be standing by. If he needs hospital treatment, then he can be flown home.'

Gina shrieked when she saw him. 'What's the matter with Ted?'

'We don't know. But the sooner we get back to the ship, the better.'

We hauled Ted Sullivan aboard and shuffled seats so that he could lie across the back seat. Three people squashed up on two seats, and I sat on the floor. If I didn't know better, I would have said Ted was drunk, but there had been no opportunity for surreptitious drinking. Even if he had carried a flask, Ted Sullivan had been with the group all the time, snapping away. I would have noticed any drinking.

Pepe drove fast. It was nerve-racking and my bottom was tingling from the bumps in the road by the time we reached the quayside. Sitting on the hard floor was no picnic. My back cringed with the effort of straightening up and getting out of the bus. I was as stiff as an old board.

Dr Skinner was waiting at the quayside, done up in waterproofs fastened up to her chin. She had a couple of extra crewmen with her and a stretcher.

'What have we got here?' she asked briskly.

'I don't really know,' I said. 'His name is Ted Sullivan. I would have said he'd been drinking, but there wasn't an opportunity to drink. He was found unconscious on the ground, and groaning, but he has come round since. He's very confused.'

'Did he fall?'

'No one saw him fall. He doesn't look as if he's had an accidental fall. No injuries, as far as I can tell. No blood, except a bruise on his forehead.'

She'd been examining him as we spoke.

She took a half-drunk bottle of mineral water from his pocket and sniffed it. Then she sniffed his breath.

'We'd better get him to the medical centre,' she said. 'Is there a Mrs Sullivan with him?'

'I don't think so. A woman called Gina was with him, but I think she's a shipboard friend.'

'Mr Sullivan? Can you hear me? I'm Dr Skinner. Can you tell me what happened?' She put her head close to his face.

'D-dunno what happened,' he groaned. At least he understood the question, even if he didn't have an answer. 'Dizzy . . . fell.'

As he spoke, he was being wrapped in a blanket and lifted onto the stretcher. It was an art getting him onto the lurching tender. But the crewmen managed it without dropping him into the water. There were the usual gawpers, and I tried to disperse them.

'Give him air, please,' I said, forming a sort of human barrier.

'Plenty of air in this gale,' said a joker.

'Is he going to be all right?' asked a subdued Gina. The lace shawl now looked like widow's weeds. Her flamboyance had gone.

'You'll be able to find out soon,' I said. 'Phone the medical centre and they'll tell you. I'm sure he's going to be fine.'

'It's the Panama Canal tomorrow. He was looking forward to seeing it and taking photographs. He's never seen it before. I've been through it at least three times myself.'

'He may well have recovered by tomorrow. A night in the medical centre may be all he needs. Why not get something warm to wear from your cabin and then go up and get some midnight snacks being served in the Boulevard Café? You could do with a hot drink or some soup.'

'I'm not hungry, but something hot to drink would be nice.' She sounded more cheerful.

Dr Skinner dismissed me as soon as we got on board. She was very good at dismissing people. There was nothing unkind about it. She had her work to do and people got in the way.

I put on a fleece and some socks, soaking up the instant warmth, then went up to the Boulevard Café to write up my report in a quiet spot. I needed something hot, too. A bowl of mushroom and garlic soup with croutons was perfect. Gina was holding court on the far side, regaling an audience with the tale of the mysterious downfall of Ted Sullivan.

'He looked absolutely awful.' Her voice carried across the café. 'Groaning.'

My report was brief and to the point. Tours Office didn't have time to read a novel. I made a quick check on the disco, but there was no need. Gary was there, playing the same music, but the bar was almost empty. It was no fun trying to boogie on a tilting floor. He winked at me.

'You could pack up early at this rate,' I said.

He nodded. 'An early night would be great.'

Early night? He called midnight an early night?

'Sweet dreams,' I said.

'You bet,' he grinned. 'I've got a few of those lined up.'

I wondered with whom; he was popular.

The *Aveline* was having a rough time, even at anchor. I could feel the pull, but the ship was firm and secure to the bed of the sea. Her size and weight were a stabilizing factor in this kind of weather.

The red light was blinking on the answer phone in my cabin. It was Dr Skinner.

'Hi, Casey. I thought you might like to know. Ted Sullivan isn't drunk. He was drugged. More tomorrow when I've made a few tests. Sweet dreams.'

Sweet dreams? They were turning into nightmares. I needed a pair of strong arms around me. But where would I find some? The only arms that I fancied were Samuel Mallory's. There was no one on board this ship that I could go to. I knew no one. I was alone.

10

Panama Canal

The Panama Canal was a miracle of engineering. Fifty-one miles cut through a land mass of jungle from the Pacific Ocean to the Atlantic. It would take the *Aveline* nine slow hours to travel along this great time-saver. We would go through three huge locks: the Miraflores, the Pedro Miguel and, after the sprawling Lake Gatún, the Gatún lock.

Shipboard events were minimal and the mysteries seemed to recede. No one was interested in anything except sitting on deck. Dozens of bags and books reserving deck loungers and an all-day canal commentary from the bridge. We were told that each year the canal handles over 1,300 ships, mostly cargo and cruise. Each ship is charged according to its tonnage. One brave man swam the length of the canal. He got charged, too. Not much, said the commentator. It worked out around a dollar a kilo.

Happily he was not devoured by crocodiles on his swim. This was spot-the-croc season. The leathery reptiles sunbathed on the banks, oblivious to the great ships creating a cooling wash.

'Ted Sullivan's bottle of water was spiked.'

It was Judith Skinner. I liked the way she appeared at my side, any time, any place, and told me straight. I was on deck as we passed under the immense Bridge of the Americas and entered the canal. We had embarked twenty Panamanian linesmen to help us through the locks. I knew what the doctor was talking about.

'Not surprised. Any idea what it was?'

'It was Midazolam, a controlled drug, but anyone working in a hospital can get hold of it. It gives the appearance of drunkenness, the sort of thing kids put in Coca Cola for a lark.'

'Is Mr Sullivan recovering?'

'Yes, he's sleeping it off. He's doing very well. He can return to the world of cruising any time. He's had a lucky escape. If he had drunk the whole bottle of drugged water, it might have been a different story.'

'Ah . . . any malicious intent?'

'Possibly, somewhere along the line. I must go. I only wanted a quick word.' Dr Skinner was already retreating.

'Thanks.'

The good doctor was gone in a puff of ether. Back to the busy medical centre, where the sick and ailing passengers awaited her attention. She didn't get much time off.

The other good doctor was still in my head. Sometimes the feeling was so strong I thought that Sam was by my side. I could hear his voice as if he had never left. I was a danger to passing traffic.

I did my goodwill tour of the decks, smiling and talking to people, pointing out things of interest. The world never ceases to fascinate me. I often get asked if sailing the same routes is boring. It's never boring because the passage of time brings change. There's always something new along the way, something I hadn't noticed before.

Gina was sunbathing in a Lurex bikini. She was a little overweight for such flimsy coverage, and her sunhat was larger than the bikini. She caught sight of me and waved me over.

'I've sent in a letter saying how wonderful you were last night, taking charge and doing everything possible to save Ted. You were so cool, calm and efficient,' she said. She was lathering herself with factor 30. 'I sent the letter to the captain. I thought he ought to know.'

'How kind,' I said. 'Thank you. I really appreciate that. We often get letters of complaint. You know, not enough ice in the free drink type of complaints.'

The letter had been addressed to the captain, thank goodness. Pierre would have shredded it.

'Is Ted all right now?' she asked.

'Yes, he's recovering, but I doubt if he'll want an alcoholic drink for a couple of days.'

'I don't know where he got the drink from. We didn't stop at any bars, did we?'

Gina wasn't aware that his bottle of water had been spiked.

'No. It was a whistle-stop tour.'

'We could both do with sticking to orange juice. Give the poor old liver a chance to recover.' She waved over a passing waiter. 'I'm going to have the recommended cocktail of the day. Panama Passion. Would you like one?' She gave her order.

I shook my head. 'No, thank you, Gina. A bit early for me. I did wonder if you knew where Mr Sullivan got his bottle of water? Do you know if he bought it on board? Or did he bring it with him from his cabin? Can you remember?'

'I think he brought it with him. It's not exactly something that one notices, is it? Water is water. We all have a couple of bottles stacked away somewhere.'

'True. I only wondered. Here comes your Panama Passion. It looks wonderful.'

It did indeed. It was festooned with a paper umbrella, slices of fruit and whisked-up alcohol, all in a blue Martini glass. She signed the chit and took her first sip through the straw. 'It is wonderful,' she sighed.

I moved on, leaving Gina to enjoy her Panama Passion. She was set to order a second. I was sure that the bar would have good sales today. Everyone was on deck. It was getting hotter. The hotter it got, the thirstier they became, the more drinks sold.

I knew the canal by heart: the number of chambers we traversed, the time they took to fill with gallons and gallons of water. We had a tug on standby for the narrowest section of the canal under the Centennial Bridge.

It was the perfect time for asking innocuous questions.

It's something the police can't do. Amateur investigators can ask the strangest questions and follow wild clues without all the encumbrance of interview rooms and statements. And all we are looking for is the truth. Leave it to the professionals to arrest, charge and try.

I roamed the decks, looking for anyone from the Queensbury quiz group. John Fletcher seemed to be absent from the bars or pools, grieving for his wife, no doubt. As unsympathetic as it may sound, I didn't feel that his grieving was all that genuine. I might be wrong. People hide their true feelings, especially men. Stiff upper lip, and all that.

But John Fletcher was not in his cabin, grieving. He was at the stern of the ship, almost unrecognizable in a floppy linen hat and dark sunglasses. He was taking photographs.

'I know what you're thinking,' he said, spotting me. 'You think it's strange, me being out here, but this is what Lorna would have wanted me to do. We had saved hard for this cruise. We had both been looking forward to it for months.'

'So why do you think she took her life?' I asked.

'I don't think she did. I don't believe it was suicide. You might say that I've read too many detective novels, but it doesn't look right to me. It wasn't like her. She was full of beans that evening. We'd been to a nice drinks party. We were all geared up towards winning the quiz and then she got this headache. Not like her at all. She was not a headachy person.'

'What do you think happened?' I asked, leaning on a rail and looking at the churning waves. I was starting to feel tired.

'I don't know. Someone or something got to her. She got a phone call. That Ted Sullivan was always giving her the eye, trying to get her to meet him on deck. He thought he was God's gift to women.'

'I take it that you don't like Ted Sullivan? Did your wife feel the same?'

'She thought he was an idiot, but a harmless idiot. She wanted him off the team because he kept making silly remarks.'

'Did you know that something unusual happened to Ted Sullivan during the Panama City tour last night?' I wasn't going to say what, but I wanted to see his reaction.

John Fletcher snorted. 'I'm not surprised. There must be a dozen husbands who would like to teach him a lesson. I hope it hurt a lot.'

Dr Skinner had told me that John Fletcher had not wanted his wife's body to be flown home. Waste of money, he'd said. He'd muttered something about a burial at sea. Cruise ships were never happy about burials at sea, as it upset the other passengers. It always took place very discreetly, late at night; a ceremony without any bands or bugles.

We had an onboard pastor for the Sunday services, and he would be there to say a few suitable words. Captain Wellington would be there, too. I'd never seen a burial at sea. It might be quite moving.

So far on this cruise, I'd had one missing person (Tracy Coleman), one suicide (Lorna Fletcher) and one attempted GBH (Ted Sullivan). It was not exactly attempted murder. Dr Skinner had not been that explicit. And then there was Henry Fellows who had not been seen since 'sleeping it off'. I didn't know how to categorize him.

And there was one entertainment director AWOL. Perhaps I ought to send him some flowers. A bunch of lilies? I left a message on his answer phone, in case he was another victim of mysterious circumstances.

'Hi, it's Casey,' I said cheerfully. 'Hope you are feeling better. Best wishes from everyone.' I refused to say that we were missing him. I'm not that good at telling lies. We were doing very well without him.

★ ★ ★

I was still no wiser, but it had been good to talk to Gina, John Fletcher and Dr Skinner. Ted Sullivan was next on my list, if I could find him. But instead, someone else unexpectedly turned up.

Debbie was back in the entertainment office. She was looking much better and had colour in her cheeks. Her hair was newly washed and shining.

'Dr Skinner has given me medication, and I'm feeling much better. Dr Skinner said it was a natural miscarriage, probably an imperfect placenta and the foetus wasn't getting any nourishment. She said it often happens with first babies. She said it was absolutely no fault of mine. It would have happened anytime, wherever I was.'

'That's good to know, isn't it? Nature's way of correcting mistakes,' I said, switching on my computer to check email. 'I still want you to take it easy. You've had a rough time. Fortunately, the canal is a light day, so no vigorous activities in demand. I'll do the two stage shows and then the quiz. Gary can do his usual disco and the karaoke. You can have the evening off.'

'Thank you, Casey. You're so thoughtful. Peter-pecker would have had me doing twice as much. I've done the programme draft for tomorrow,' she said. 'It's a day at sea, so chock-a-block full of talks and games, line dancing, pottery. I could hardly get them all in.'

'That's a real help, thanks. We'll do a quick check together and then we can send it down to the printers.'

There was an email from Edmund Morgan. He sounded agitated.

'*Hi Casey. I hope you don't mind. I'm really worried by the escalation of events. It's getting out of control. Perhaps it's time to call in the cavalry. You have your job to do and I have mine. We can't expect miracles and this is all beyond me. Edmund.'*

I emailed back, short and sweet. 'Sound the bugle.'

I didn't know what he meant, and it didn't really matter. I had suspected it was getting too much for him. His Marine background might have been sedentary; the payroll office would suit him.

Next were some emails from Head Office. I answered them in my name, without saying that Pierre had taken extended sick leave, hoping they would put two and two together and come up with five.

We were entering Gatún Lake for our transit and taken on the twenty Panamanian linesmen again. Their job was to secure us to the mules at each end of the ship. The mules were not stubborn, four-legged creatures with nasty tempers, but instead very powerful engines on tracks. We had four mules at each end, and once they were in position, they pulled the ship into the first chamber. Once we were lowered down to the level of the next chamber, they could move us forward, then switch back and repeat it all over again. It was a long process. Three chambers of water to transverse in total, keenly watched by most of the passengers.

It was an eerie process if you were sitting in one of the lounges. The walls of the lock chamber would rise up, only inches from the windows, and it would go almost dark.

I went up on deck. We were going through the breakwaters that marked the end of the Panama Canal. Our course now moved through the Bahia Limon and across the Colombian Basin towards the Dutch Antilles.

I was leaning on the rail, letting the bracing sea air blow away the sultriness of the long land-bound transit. There was a movement by my side, but I did not stir, pretending not to notice. The Atlantic Ocean was mesmerizing, its colour so dark, the waves so powerful, the white horses, wild and furious.

'So this is how you spend your time, is it? Is the entertainment department running on autopilot while you take in the views? I'm surprised, Casey Jones. You are usually so dedicated to your job.'

I knew that amused voice. I did not have to turn round. My heart turned over in a double somersault.

'Detective Chief Inspector Bruce Everton,' I breathed. 'What are you doing here? Surely not a stowaway? We don't allow stowaways, you know. They get chucked into the brig.'

He chuckled. 'It might be an improvement on the cabin I've been allocated, somewhere down on Z deck. The ship's pretty full, I'm told. There are only a few empty cabins.'

'I'm glad you're here. You're a godsend. I hope you don't mind being drawn into the security chaos that is, at present, on board the *Aveline*.'

'So I understand.'

This was the cavalry. DCI Bruce Everton from Scotland Yard. I had no idea what strings had been pulled to get him on board, but I was pleased. I knew I could rely on this man. He was a tower of strength.

11

At Sea

Detective Chief Inspector Bruce Everton was once my rock, my stave from an earlier cruise on the *Countess Georgina*. He had been brought on board then to deal with a tragic set of circumstances.

'I'm really pleased to see you,' I said again, trying not to show my pleasure too much. I liked him; he was a good man. 'But why have you been summoned, if that's the right word? We don't exactly have a homicide on our hands.'

'That's true. No mutilated corpse or manic murderer. But you do have one woman in an icebox who should not be there.'

'Lorna Fletcher, you mean? Did Edmund tell you that? Surely the ship's grapevine doesn't have wings?'

'Who's Edmund? Yes, Lorna Fletcher, John Fletcher's wife. John is convinced that she didn't commit suicide and that somehow it was made to look like suicide. He phoned me from the ship and asked me to take a look in to the circumstances. He doesn't know that you lead a double life and how ingenious you are sometimes, that you had probably come to the same conclusion.'

So this was not Edmund calling in the cavalry.

'He thinks you work hard, and are a very beautiful woman wearing a succession of gorgeous clothes.' Bruce nodded and grinned.

'How kind.' It sounded trite, but I was touched. 'So how did you get here, if it wasn't Edmund? How was it all arranged?'

Bruce Everton still had a weary look about him. It had probably been a terrible journey. 'I flew out to Panama City, arrived very late last night and had a horrendously rough boat ride out to the ship which was anchored in the harbour. I've been sleeping it off since. It was really good news to find that you were also on the *Aveline*,' he added with a smile.

'So you are not here officially?'

'No, not yet. But it could become official. I'm taking a well-earned holiday, one leg of the cruise only, as a guest of John Fletcher. I hope to repay his generosity by solving the mystery of his wife's death.'

'We will, we will,' I said, suddenly full of optimism. We could do anything together.

'I shall need to see the . . . body,' he said. He hesitated over the word.

'I can arrange that with Dr Skinner.'

'Your ship's doctor may have missed something. GPs are not usually trained in forensics.'

Bruce Everton was a good-looking man, quite a bit older than me. But age was easy to forget in his company. His thick, greyish hair looked distinguished. His lean body was the pay-off from many hours in the gym and would look good in any state of undress. But we had never got that far. It had been a genuine friendship, touched by the occasional sexual frisson.

'So how do you know John Fletcher? And how does he know you? What's the background here?'

Bruce looked disconcerted. 'Don't laugh, Casey. It's the old story. We play golf together.'

'Golf is no laughing matter, I understand,' I said, keeping a straight face.

'You are laughing. I knew you would. You think it's funny, grown men hitting a tiny white ball around acres of green grass and into a distant hole.'

'I'm sure it gives you a great deal of pleasure, though I have never actually understood the complexities of the game.' Straight face still in place.

'Also John Fletcher is a retired policeman. He was never plain clothes or CID, but a copper on the beat. Now does that make more sense?'

'Of course, that makes perfect sense: the police network. He was quite right to get you on board. You're the best. Now, let's go sort out your dismal cabin.'

★   ★   ★

It was the worst cabin I had ever seen, situated at the far end of the crew deck, fathoms below sea level. Four narrow bunk beds with a heavy black TV on a tiny cabinet placed in between them. There was no chair, no table, no telephone, no fridge, no tea-making facilities, no chest of drawers. The so-called bathroom was a corner partitioned off with a shower and a tiny washbasin. No towel rail, not even a mug for his toothbrush.

The carpet needed a steam clean. The shower curtain was stained with urine. Graffiti was scrawled on the walls. The only touch of value was a twenty-two-inch-long shelf, if you could call that an amenity.

'This is awful, Bruce,' I said. 'I'm so ashamed and so sorry. You can't stay here. There must have been a terrible mistake. I didn't know such squalor existed on this ship. Even the crew shouldn't have to put up with this.'

'I thought I was being downgraded for some devious reason.'

'Who said this was your cabin? I'd like to find out who put you here.'

'Some cadet met me off the tender and escorted me to this cabin. I don't know who it was. It was pretty dark and I was dead tired. I didn't even bother to unpack.' His soft case was on the floor, still strapped up.

'Well, they certainly didn't want you to stay. I think it was deliberate. No one would stay in these circumstances. They thought you would get off at the next port of call. Let's see what the purser can find for you.'

★ ★ ★

The purser was apologetic. 'I'm really sorry this has happened, Mr Everton. There has been a terrible mistake. You were taken there by accident by a very new cadet. Your cabin is 104 A deck, next to John Fletcher. I'll get a steward to move your things immediately.'

'I didn't unpack,' said Bruce.

'How did this happen?' I persisted. 'Don't you know why the cadet escorted Mr Everton to that crew cabin?'

'I'll make enquiries and let you know what I discover.' Purser-speak for 'no comment'.

'Thank you,' I said. 'I shall be interested to know. So will Captain Wellington. Mr Everton is a personal friend.'

What a whopper. I'd make sure they became friends as soon as possible.

I took Bruce up to the Boulevard Café, which was fast becoming my favourite rendezvous. Bruce collected a tray full of delicious bits and pieces while I got two cups of tea. I remembered how he liked it. We found a table out of earshot of any passengers and I filled him in on the events of the past few days. I left nothing out, not even Pierre Arbour's undisguised dislike of me.

'I get all the worst jobs, constant put-downs and sometimes direct rudeness. He is not my favourite person.'

'It's jealousy,' said Bruce. 'Sheer jealousy because you are good at your job, probably better than him, and much better-looking. Remember your ten commandments. No one can beat you.' He selected a canapé of toast piled high with prawns. 'You're the tops.'

'You're the Eiffel Tower,' I sang back.

'Sorry, that's all I know of that song.'

'Don't forget to leave room for tonight's supper,' I said, amused by his hunger. 'Dozens of delicious courses designed to be consumed in a short time.'

'I may not have time for supper,' he said. 'There's a lot to do and I must see John Fletcher straight away. All these mysterious happenings on one cruise and within days of each other. I can't help but wonder if they are linked.'

'Tracy Coleman, Lorna Fletcher and Ted Sullivan? And there's Henry Fellows. I keep saying 'and Henry Fellows' as if he's an afterthought. No one seems to know anything about him. It would be strange indeed. A more unlikely foursome one could hardly imagine. I must go and change for tonight. Sorry, Bruce, work calls. I'll see you later.'

'How about a nightcap somewhere?'

'Perfect.' If I could find him again . . .

It would have to be my black fishtail chiffon tonight, as a sign of respect for Lorna Fletcher. No gaudy glad rags, no razzmatazz. I'd also asked Debbie to wear something discreet when introducing the

Russian concert pianist. We had both suddenly remembered the concert and Debbie said she could do it, as long as she sat down most of the time.

'Time to go get dolled up,' Bruce said, eyeing up some egg and salad canapé, wrapped in pastry. He probably hadn't eaten decently for days. One day I would ask him if there was a Mrs Everton, but did I want to know? Cruise ships were a kind of no-man's-land. 'I'll catch you around for a late-night drink.'

'It'll be very late,' I warned. 'I'm short of staff. The passengers will be keen for all sorts of entertainment after going cross-eyed watching for crocs all day. But I'm really glad you're here. I was beginning to feel lost and isolated.' I didn't mention feeling alarmed and a bit frightened.

'That's the nicest thing anyone has said to me for years,' said Bruce. This time he was not looking at me. Perhaps he was afraid of what his eyes might be saying. 'And I like the sound of being very late. I'm at my best when being very late. Police training.'

I liked the sound of it, too.

* * *

The two shows tonight were hour-long tributes to the genius of Ivor Novello and his music. Rather before my time, but the lovely songs had lived on.

It was such a big theatre, there was no way I could see who was sitting in the audience. But I did notice that Ted Sullivan was circulating again, back in hunter-gatherer mode, bottled water in hand. I hoped he'd checked the seal. Gina was nowhere to be seen. Perhaps she had moved on to fresher, lusher pastures.

It was getting rough outside. I wondered how the dancers managed to keep their balance on that stage. They wore high heels, but always with a T-strap to keep the shoe secure. I heard drinks sliding off tables. We were riding rough weather.

Chief Engineer Daniel Webster was hurrying along the promenade deck, done up in his waterproofs. I was taking a breather between shows.

'Better stay inside, Casey,' he said. 'Time to batten down the hatches.'

'Is it going to get that bad?'

'No, not at all,' he said cheerfully. 'Maybe a bit blustery.'

It was more than a bit blustery. I was no novice sailor. The *Aveline* was rocking, hit by waves and a wind that was force nine or ten. I could feel the old *Aveline* groaning inside the new hull, absorbing the battering. I made the precarious journey to the IT room and via a hurried Google search, found the weather forecast for this leg of the cruise.

And the news wasn't good.

Hurricane Ricky. The meteorological office had precise details. We were heading into the path of Hurricane Ricky. Surely Captain Wellington had time to plot a different route or head inland for some safe harbour? A ship should never argue with a hurricane.

Maybe Hurricane Ricky had changed course, unpredictable and precocious as hurricanes always are. But I didn't like the sound of it. Hurricanes could be dangerous aboard a big ship. It would be prudent to cancel the quiz, otherwise papers and drinks would be flying all over the place. Passengers would be safer in their cabins, watching the replay of an old film. And I had my team to consider.

Edmund Morgan was hurrying forward, wearing his worried look. 'Don't go outside, Casey. No stargazing tonight.'

'But I love my stargazing.'

'Not safe.'

'Are we really heading into the path of Hurricane Ricky?' I asked.

'Good heavens, wherever did you get that idea?' he blustered. 'It's just a bit of a gale.'

After the second Ivor Novello show, which was understandably not well attended, I began searching the bars for Bruce Everton. I'd feel safer beside him, in just a bit of a gale.

Food. Where had food gone to? I couldn't remember my last food intake. I'd missed dinner by doing both shows.

Romanoff Petrik cannoned into me as I left the Acropolis Theatre, on my way to make sure that no one turned up for the quiz. It had been cancelled over the tannoy and on the in-cabin television. The disco had also been cancelled. The casino stayed open in any weather. The serious punters were oblivious to the weather.

'Please, Miss Jones, Miss Casey, for one minute. You are the only one I can talk to. I must talk to you.'

The Russian pianist looked distraught, his dark hair dishevelled, white shirt buttoned up the wrong way, black bow tie unfastened. His concert had also been cancelled and maybe he was at a loose end. I had not seen him for ages. He was always practising, for hours every day.

'Sure,' I said. 'Let's find somewhere we can safely sit.'

'You don't understand. Nobody understands.'

'That's true,' I agreed. 'And no one will understand unless you tell me what you are talking about. Let's sit here and you can tell me what you are worried about.'

It was a pair of armchairs, selectively placed outside the art gallery where the art connoisseurs could look through the wares on show. But tonight there would be no one there.

'Tracy Coleman. Why is no one looking

for her? They all say that she left the ship in Acapulco, but she didn't. Why is no one checking her swipe card? It will show she never left the ship. She is still here. She never got off.' His voice was trembling with passion.

'She never got off? How do you know that?' I asked. 'How can you be so sure? Everyone says she went ashore at Acapulco.'

'Because she was with me all day,' said Romanoff, wringing his priceless, highly insured hands. 'We were in bed, my bed, making love. We were in bed the whole day. Tracy and me, we are desperately in love. We are having a shipboard romance, an affair. But now she has disappeared and I cannot find her anywhere.'

He did look distraught, his deep brown eyes clouded with worry.

'But you have said something to someone, surely?'

'Yes, I have asked many people, but everyone says she went ashore and did not come back.'

'You've told them that she was with you?'

He shook his head, dark hair falling over his eyes. 'No, I have not said this. It was not right, you see. I have a wife in Moscow. She would be very upset, my Natasha. I must protect her. We married very young.'

Another tangled web, these shipboard romances. But if Tracy Coleman was still on board, where was she? She could be trapped or being held prisoner, or lying injured in some desolate spot. A chill touched my spine. She could have been pushed overboard as we left Acapulco, weighted down, and was even now on the seabed of the harbour.

'Have you ever been to her cabin?'

'No, never. I don't even know where it is. She always came to my cabin.'

'It's been wrecked — clothes, make-up, everything. But her inhaler, for asthma, is still there among the debris.'

His face lightened a degree. 'There, that proves it. She always took her inhaler with her. She is still on the ship. We must find her.' Suddenly his face went white under his tan. 'Oh my God, she may not be alive. Something may have happened to her. Please, Miss Jones, you believe me, don't you? You're a nice lady, with a kind face. Help me find her.'

No one had ever said I had a kind face before. 'I believe you. Yes, I'll do what I can. I'll get the security officer, Edmund Morgan, to organize a thorough search of the ship, all the storerooms, the laundry, the kitchens, everywhere. Even the engine rooms. Try not to worry.'

'But I am worried. She is so beautiful, so vivacious, such a lovely person. I cannot bear anything to have happened to her.'

I'd seen the photograph of Tracy Coleman in the entertainment team group on the wall outside the library. She was tall and willowy with lots of dark, wavy hair and sparkling eyes. Quite a glamorous woman. It was no wonder the romantic Russian had been taken by her looks.

'Did everyone like her?'

'Oh yes, she was very popular, always laughing and joking. Maybe some of the ladies were a little jealous, but she never did anything wrong.'

Except with you, I thought. Though perhaps Romanoff had not mentioned Mrs Petrik. Some men do forget these details.

'Was there anyone who did not like her?'

Romanoff snorted in a loud, emphatic way. 'Did not like her? I tell you, this man hated her. He made her life a number-one bad misery. She said that one day, she would lose her temper and kill him.'

'And who was that?' I asked quietly, wondering if I already knew the answer. Of course, I did.

'I keep out of his way, or I would kill him, too. Fast, with a knife. He is, as you say, a smarmy lizard. The director of entertainment, Monsieur Pierre Arbour. He is making my darling Tracy into this mystery.'

His English was garbled, but I understood.

12

Hurricane Ricky

A rough sea and a gale-force wind should be nothing to a fine modern ship like the *Countess Aveline*. The wind whistled through lines and along corridors and the waves slapped the hull with relentless fury as we rode the Caribbean Sea.

I'd been on the edge of a hurricane before, but it had never been this bad. Walking was a calculated hazard: forget pride; hold on to everything handy. The crew was busy putting up extra ropes across open spaces of carpet. The Zanzibar Dining Room had closed, and I could see the staff hurriedly stacking cutlery and glassware into secure compartments.

My flimsy evening dress was not the right gear for a hurricane. I'd get blown away. The stairs were too dangerous, so I took the lift down to my cabin and

189

changed into a tracksuit and trainers. I also grabbed a lightweight waterproof jacket. We were pitching and rolling.

'Nothing to worry about,' Edmund Morgan said again, when I phoned him. 'It's only a tropical disturbance. We don't get hurricanes of any magnitude in this area, believe me.'

'It seems pretty rough to me,' I said. 'I can't understand why we aren't going towards the land, to some safe harbour. All the captains I've known have always taken the safest route. They daren't do anything else.'

'Perhaps Captain Wellington thinks our extra speed will outride the hurricane.'

'There. I knew it was a hurricane. Hurricane Ricky. Edmund, I want to see you. Can we talk somewhere?'

'You should stay in your cabin and watch a movie. It'll blow itself out by the morning. Goodnight, Casey.'

'This is important. It's about Tracy Coleman.'

'What about Tracy Coleman?'

I knew a little about hurricanes. I knew there was a vortex, the centre, where all was calm. In a quadrant, the ship could be sucked in or buffeted out, like a spinning top. But the *Aveline* was far too big to suffer such treatment. The captain was probably, even now, plotting our escape route. We would be in radio contact with all the shore stations.

But hurricane behaviour is eccentric. It can change course, change velocity and change strength in minutes. Still, at least a big ship is safer than a building. Bungalows and offices get torn down. Palm trees flattened. Cars wrecked and tossed about.

'I have got to see you,' I said. I'd read somewhere that the spin of the earth is what starts hurricanes, that and hot and cold air; that a hurricane is a vast energy produced by the condensation of water from rising air. A little bit of knowledge is always confusing.

The strength of the wind was increasing. I could feel it buffeting my cabin window, waves obliterating any night-time view. It would be safer to stay here and tuck myself up with a hot chocolate and a good book. I was about to change my mind when Edmund agreed to meet me.

'I'll meet you at the north end of the Cairo Lounge,' said Edmund. 'Take the lift. Don't take the stairs. They are too dangerous. You could get thrown down.'

Everything was being battened down. On deck, the crew were lashing down all the loungers. The cushions were being stacked inside. The deck bars were closed, shutters down. The pool was being covered with heavy tarpaulin and lashed down.

A few passengers were about, hoping for something spectacular to video. The gamblers were still working the fruit machines and tables in the casino. They hadn't even noticed that it was rough.

The Cairo Lounge was deserted, and I soon spotted Edmund. He was sitting at a table in a corner with two glasses, each one a third full of golden liquid which was slopping about inside the glass.

'Thought you might like a brandy,' he said.

'Thank you,' I said, sitting down carefully. 'That's really thoughtful of you. Definitely brandy weather.'

'I hope this is good,' he said. 'I've got other things to do.'

There was a loud shriek of wind, turning to a low roaring sound. I could see fast fans of water against the lounge windows. It was frightening. I turned away, hoping the windows would hold out against the force. They must use extra-strong double-glazing — treble-glazing maybe. The familiar sea waves and sea spray had gone. Instead we were surrounded by mountains of water, sucking back its own foam.

I shuddered. I am not frightened of the sea and can cope with bad weather, but this was something different. My ten commandments were being no help. I should have been comforting passengers, but they had all vanished.

'I have some information about Tracy Coleman which could mean that she is still on board, trapped somewhere or being held prisoner. Maybe she has fallen and is injured. We need a full-on ship search, every nook and cranny.'

'Hardly possible now, Casey.'

'I didn't say now, at this very moment.'

'Who wants this search?'

'It's Romanoff Petrik, the Russian pianist. He says that she did not go ashore at Acapulco. He is very sure.'

'Romeo Romanoff? Him? Why should he say that?'

'Because Tracy was with him, all day. They were in bed.'

'Ah.' Edmund gulped at his brandy. 'A little romance?'

'A big romance, I think. Fairly serious. He is very worried.'

The older and smaller *Aveline* creaked inside her new modern hull, as if remembering other battles with the sea. She had been seaworthy for years, totalling thousands of nautical miles without a mishap. Some tables slid across the dance floor and the heavy armchairs inched in different directions, bumping into each other like bumper cars on fairground dodgems.

The wind speed was immense, sending spray like fountains over the ship. We couldn't see anything out the windows. I ought to have checked on the safety of my staff. Debbie, Gary, even Pierre. I got

Debbie on my mobile.

'We're barricaded up in the disco bar,' said Debbie. 'It's too dangerous to take the short outside walk to the lifts. Can't hear the music, though. Turn up the volume, Gary.'

'Will you be all right?'

'Sure. No one can stand up without holding on. It's a bit like a roller-coaster ride. Half the off-duty officers are up here. Best view of any, they said.'

'I should think they'll all be back on duty any moment, if this gets any worse. What about Pierre?'

'If I know Pierre, he has taken a strong sleeping pill with a double whisky and is snoring it off in his bed.'

'Is it worth a call to check?'

'Don't expect any answer.'

There wasn't one.

'Have you any idea who met Bruce Everton when he came on board at Panama City?' I said suddenly to Edmund.

'Bruce Everton? Who's he? Have we got an extra passenger? How unusual for this leg. One of the stewards, probably.'

His face was quite blank. 'I'd better go.'

I phoned Judith Skinner down in the depths. 'Are you busy? I'm wondering if you need any help,' I said. 'I can't do anything medical, but I can talk reassuringly to your patients and hold a hand.'

'Bless you. We could do with your help down here,' said Judith. 'Brittle bones break like straw in weather like this. And we have so many falls. I can find you something to do, even if it's only making cups of tea. But take care on the way, Casey. We don't want another casualty.'

Edmund Morgan had gone, hopefully to initiate some kind of search for Tracy Coleman, but I realized that people had other things on their mind during Hurricane Ricky. The ship was taking a battering, constantly hit by huge waves. Except for a few lulls, you could not see anything, not even the sea. It was still frightening, but I was beginning to feel that we would soon emerge into calmer water.

I took the lift down to the medical centre. Thank goodness the lifts were working. The corridors were eerily empty.

196

Most of the passengers had taken refuge in their cabins, as instructed, preferring to be tossed about in a small area that was familiar and raiding the minibar in the lulls.

The medical centre was full. A lot of passengers had fallen and hurt themselves, some badly, some only bruised and shocked. The waiting room was full. Chief nurse Helen gave me a clipboard with forms to fill in. It was something I could do even when the floor was tilting. Some of the women were crying. I offered tissues and words of comfort. I couldn't calm the waves.

Down here we could not hear the howling of the hurricane, only feel it. We could only guess at the concentration of the officers on the bridge, this great ship shuddering in their hands. The wind was continuing to increase. It was now a solid roar which echoed in the confined space.

Bruce Everton came through the door to the medical centre. Windswept was not a strong enough word. He was wind-battered, flattened. He'd never encountered such weather and his ashen face said so.

'This is not my idea of luxury cruising,' he gasped, holding on to the receptionist's desk. 'I thought yesterday was rough enough.'

'It'll soon be over,' I said hopefully.

'I'm beginning to wish I'd stayed at home,' he said. 'One night without sleep was enough. This looks like being another sleepless night. Casey, are you all right? I heard you were down here.'

'I'm all right, but we could do with your strong arm. We can't get these ladies safely along to X-ray. Can you help? Mrs Wells first, please. She has a really nasty sprain.'

'Come along, Mrs Wells. Let's get you sorted,' Bruce said. His smile was warm, reassuring. I felt safe with him. So did Mrs Wells.

★   ★   ★

The hurricane continued to increase, though we could barely hear anything of the wind or the sea over the continual roar. The wind force could have been over the Beaufort scale. I had no way of knowing. All I could do was give some kind of assistance to those who were hurt or injured. Reception had been handing out free seasickness pills to anyone who made it to the deck.

But a corner of my mind was thinking about Tracy Coleman. Where was she in all this? I hoped she was safe and not being thrown about in some insecure hold. How were we ever going to find her?

We lost track of time. Relays of tea and coffee arrived from somewhere, mugs rattling on tilted trays, sliding as the ship rolled. Our decks were immensely strong and made to withstand the suction of the wind. But the hatches were more vulnerable. They could cope with force from above, but pressure from a different angle and they could give way. The crew was dealing with deluges of water.

Cabin doors were jamming and the maintenance crews were hurrying about to emergency calls. Passengers were imprisoned inside or outside their cabins. Pictures began to hang askew or come loose. The art gallery stock was all over the place and the staff were trying to save their valuable wares from destruction.

The medical centre had less panic than other areas of the ship. Passengers in the medical centre knew that they had been hurt or injured and were resigned to their fate. They'd arrived for treatment and were getting it. Elsewhere on board, passengers were trying not to fall or be blown over. No broken bones and having to be flown home for them, thank you. Only the gamblers seemed oblivious to the mayhem outside.

'A bit blowy,' one of them said, looking up from the spinning wheel.

I was surprised when Edmund appeared in the entrance to the medical centre. I was trying to work out what to do for a woman who had bashed her elbow on a wall. Edmund was done up to the neck in waterproofs, and he was dripping water onto the floor, his hair wet and flattened.

'Can I talk to you, Casey?' he mouthed.

I nodded and passed the patient on to a nurse for an ice compress.

'What is it?' I asked.

'You aren't going to like this.'

'I don't particularly like anything about this evening. This is not my favourite way of ending the day. What is the time? We've lost track down here.'

'It's past midnight. Well past, nearly one a.m. We should run out of this weather by dawn. You are safer down here.'

He was blinking the water off his eyelashes. He could barely see. The water was dripping off his nose.

'Tell me what you want to tell me,' I said, leading him to an empty chair. To hell with the cost of the upholstery. The man was drenched. Take it out of my salary.

'It's Tracy Coleman,' he said, helping himself to my mug of coffee. 'The hurricane, you know.'

'Yes, Tracy?'

'We've found her.'

A wave of relief, a dry one, washed over me. Romanoff Petrik had been right. Tracy had not been left behind in Acapulco, as everyone thought. She had been here, all the time, on board the ship.

'Good,' I said. 'How is she?'

'She's dead.'

13

At Sea

Tracy Coleman had been found in the hull of one of the small, antique lifeboats, the type from the original *Aveline*, which had not been demolished or removed for nostalgic reasons. Tracy lay like a rag doll and had been dead for several days. There was a large fracture at the back of her head. She was fully clothed and lying under a heavy folded tarpaulin. The high wind had disturbed her shroud and tipped the lifeboat.

There was a back way into the medical centre and crew members brought Tracy to the mortuary on a stretcher, away from the eyes of curious or nervous passengers.

'The dead will have to wait,' Judith Skinner said briskly, as she came out of the X-ray room. 'I've the living to look after.'

'It's one of the crew. One of the

entertainment team.'

'I know. Don't think I'm not sorry, but she'll have to wait.'

Detective Chief Inspector Everton had immediately taken charge on Captain Wellington's orders and Edmund did not seem to mind. Murder was out of his depth, and he was only too pleased to leave it all to someone else.

'Shall I tell Romanoff?' I asked, already knowing the answer.

'No,' said Bruce. 'We won't tell anyone yet. Of course, I shall keep the captain informed. And it will be difficult to stop the crew from talking among themselves, but the less anyone else knows, the better. This looks like murder.'

'Poor Tracy,' I said. 'I never knew her, but I seem to know a lot about her. I feel I know her. And I'm her replacement. Should that worry me?'

'Watch your head,' said Bruce.

Not exactly helpful or reassuring, but he knew instantly that his flippant remark had jarred. He did not touch me, but it was as if he nearly did. He came over and put his head close to mine. His eyes showed concern.

'Sorry, Casey. Murder always has that effect on me. It blunts the sensitivity. It's the only way I can deal with sudden and unnecessary death.'

'I understand,' I said. I was trying to understand.

'I've seen so many horrific sights.'

'Don't worry, Bruce. I'll be all right. You get on with what you have to do. It's in your court now.'

'May I see you back to your cabin for what is left of the night, when you have finished being Florence Nightingale without a candle or a bonnet? We can't have you falling over and breaking something vital.'

'Thank you. I'll wait here for you.'

It was a long wait. Nothing desperate had happened to our engines. They were efficient, modern, high-powered engines, ready to cope with any weather. Chief Engineer Daniel Webster could feel the stress but knew they could cope. He found time to phone me on his mobile. He had reduced speed to seven knots.

'How are you doing?' he asked.

'Coping. I'm helping out in the medical centre.'

'Good for you. Don't worry, Casey,' he said. 'We'll get through this hurricane. She's a big ship.'

'Are you working somewhere dangerous?'

He laughed. 'Not your problem, sweetheart. The air-conditioning is holding out. Not like years ago when steam heat could have killed. But take care moving around the ship. We must be coming to the vortex soon. It's a lull when it's safe to move, but it doesn't last long.'

'Thank you for phoning. Shall I see you soon?'

'Of course. It's the island of Curaçao tomorrow, when we get there. We might be a bit late. Lovely place. Dutch, you know. Very picturesque. We could have a drink at a quayside café, watch the world go by.'

It sounded so civilized, I almost forgot the hurricane outside. I nodded as if it was a video-call. But he had switched off. He had more important things to do.

Bruce came for me, some hours later. He had registered the formalities, received official permission to stay on board and was now on autopilot of fatigue. Most of the walking wounded had been escorted back to their cabins, and others had been bedded down in the small private side rooms of the medical centre.

'You need sleep now,' he said, putting his hand under my arm to steady me. I was almost too tired to stand up. I could have slept in that hard chair.

I had forgotten the fierceness of the wind, and there had been no sign of abatement. Gusts came howling, too loud for us to speak. We were too tired to talk, anyway. Suddenly it stopped; all was eerily calm. We had reached the vortex.

'Hurry,' said Bruce. 'This is the time to move. Let's get you to your cabin. D deck, 333, isn't it?'

'You've done your homework.'

'Don't talk, just walk.'

He had my hand and we moved together along the corridors. I vaguely recognized the length of D deck. It seemed years since I had been there. We stopped outside 333. Hardly the right moment to invite someone in for coffee.

Then it happened. It was electricity. His arms were round me and his mouth warm on mine was like nothing I had ever experienced before. I stood entranced, my hands by my side. I did not have the strength to lift them.

'Oh, Casey,' he sighed. 'I've been wanting to do this since the first moment I saw you. It's been a torment.'

I couldn't speak. My wits had scattered.

All sorts of quivers went through my body and my groin. I longed for him. But we were in the middle of a hurricane and romance was way down on my list. But I would remember that kiss till the end of my living days.

'Goodnight, Casey,' he said, when at last he drew away. I leaned against him, savouring the solid strength of the man. 'Good morning, I mean. Get some sleep. We both need it.'

He took my key card from me and opened the door of my cabin. It was a foreign place with things strewn all over the floor. I didn't recognize any of it or remember what happened next. The door closed and Bruce was gone. I fell onto my bed and into sleep, the sleep of the exhausted, plunging deep in to my own ocean.

★　★　★

DCI Everton was present when Dr Skinner made her first examination of Tracy Coleman. She had been dead three or four days, the doctor said. Probable cause of death: a blow to the head by a blunt instrument.

They came out of the medical centre together, faces grim, holding on to the walls. They had no idea if the storm was abating. It still felt rough.

'But it's rare that a single blow is enough to kill,' said Dr Skinner. 'Death from a brain injury can happen without the skull being fractured. Sometimes hours or even days can pass before death.'

'Do you know what kind of blunt instrument?' I asked. A couple of hours' sleep had given me a new burst of energy.

But I couldn't stay for long. I had to get my team working again to keep the passengers amused. A few passengers were up and about, determined to keep vertical and get their money's worth.

'It could have been anything. A poker, stone, rock, golf club. Anything heavy enough can be used. Even a can of beans is enough. But it doesn't always kill. Sometimes, victims are finished off some other way,' said Bruce. 'Strangulation or a knife.'

I didn't want to think about it. 'Any similarities to Lorna Fletcher's death?' I asked. I don't know what made me ask it. Two deaths on one cruise. I didn't want to connect them, but my brain had its own ideas.

'Funny you should ask,' said Judith. 'There was something. A very slight thing, but it struck me as odd.' She clamped her mouth shut. She was not going to tell me in front of Bruce Everton until she was sure.

That special kiss might never have happened. Perhaps I had dreamed it. Perhaps I'd had some weird storm hallucination due to atmospheric conditions. Bruce showed no sign of remembering it, either, but he did have his policeman's face on, and the two did not mix.

I certainly wasn't going to let Bruce see that our encounter had affected me so deeply. 'Guess I had better sort out which items I can rescue for today's programme. It had better be good. I've a hurricane to beat.'

There was no shelter outside. The wind and seas were still too rough. Everything would have to be indoors, seated. Safety first. I took the lift up to the Boulevard Café. The breakfast service was restricted. No hot dishes. It was fruit, cereal or rolls. Stewards were helping the brave, or the desperately hungry, to tables, carrying their trays.

No piles of food this morning. The less, the better. Spillage was rife. Bananas don't roll. Nor do croissants. I was hungry and thirsty. I let a steward carry my cup of coffee.

'Thank you so much,' I said.

'Rough enough for you, Miss Jones?' It

was Ted Sullivan, looking spruce and dapper, red cravat in place. He was taking the hurricane in his stride, if a little unsteadily.

'Soon be out of it,' I said. 'We are past the worst.'

'Can I have that in writing?'

'Sure, when we reach the Dutch Antilles. It's a very picturesque island. Have you been there before?'

A sudden gust sent his tray flying. Stewards rushed to clear the debris and mop up the floor. 'I was wondering if we'll get there at all. Does the captain know what he's doing?'

'We survived the night, didn't we? The storm is easing down. We are coming out of it.'

'More quiz games today?'

'A scrabble tournament, I thought. Travel scrabble. Less chance of losing the pieces. And a music quiz. Just sit and listen and hold on to your chair.'

'I like the idea of that.'

Gina appeared, looking the worse for wear, blue shadows under her eyes. Her shirt was incorrectly buttoned as if she had not been looking. She had certainly had a disturbed night, hardly sleeping, no one to hold on to. She found a wan smile for Ted Sullivan.

'So where were you when I needed you?' she asked bluntly.

'Looking after number one.'

'I should have known.'

I left them to bicker over a pecan Danish pastry. They looked as if they were enjoying it. Some people have a strange taste for what passes for enjoyment.

Both Debbie and Gary were in the office, trying to sort papers and pens which had succumbed to the violence of the storm. They both looked pale, uniforms dishevelled. Neither appeared to have had much sleep.

'I suppose you'll be expecting us to be jolly and hearty all day,' said Debbie, whose idea of tidying was putting everything jumbled into a filing tray.

'Yes, and there is work to do. Too late to print off a programme, so everything will be announced over the tannoy. The art gallery staff has agreed to do a lecture on modern paintings and Gary, will you put together a music quiz? All different kinds of music, please. Not non-stop pop or heavy rock.'

'There's a tape somewhere,' he said. 'I saw it lurking. Nearly threw it in the bin. A recording of a radio musical quiz.'

'Perfect. Find it and use it,' I said. 'No one will sue us in the middle of a hurricane. We'll plead emotional emergency.'

'Give me something easy to do,' said Debbie, holding her head in her hands.

'Travel scrabble tournament in the library after coffee time. Set up groups, read the rules and start them off. Bottle of wine for the winner. You should be done in an hour.'

'Wonderful. I can put my head down. I need some sleep.'

'Don't bank on it,' I grinned. 'I'm thinking up new amusements for the afternoon. I'll have a word with our lecturers and see if they have a spare talk.'

'How about a crochet tournament?'

'Along those lines.'

At least it made them laugh. I needed

my team to laugh. We had all forgotten about Pierre Arbour, but suddenly he was standing in the doorway. He was in well-creased white trousers, white shirt and Conway blazer, his eyes like granite.

'This is no time for fun and games,' he said. 'You are supposed to be working. I suppose you have been taking it easy while I've been ill.'

'We are still in rough weather,' I said. 'Everything closed down last night.'

'The entertainment department never closes down,' he said, striding round to my side of the desk. 'Let's see today's programme.'

'There isn't one,' I said.

'There's isn't one?' He looked about to explode. Debbie got up and hurried over to the copying machine. She pretended to print out the scrabble rules. 'What absolute nonsense, Casey. Do you mean to say you haven't produced a programme? What on earth have you been doing?'

'We were riding Hurricane Ricky all last night. Everything had to be cancelled on captain's orders,' I added. 'Half the passengers are not around this morning; they are still in their cabins. We have laid on some fairly safe and sedate games and quizzes for them. I'm about to reschedule the film shows, so that there are different films showing non-stop, all day in the cinema.'

'This is totally unacceptable, Casey, and I shall report your inefficiency to Head Office. What incompetence and lack of motivation. Scrap everything you have arranged, and we'll redo the programme from scratch.'

I could feel my patience stretching. The man had no idea of what we had gone through.

'But, Pierre, it's an excellent programme, given that we are still in rough waters,' said Gary, who earned a lot of gold stars with his instant support. 'Lots of sensible and safe activities.'

'Nonsense. You are as lazy as Casey is incompetent. Wait till you hear what I have lined up for you all. And get me some coffee, Casey. Strong and black. It's all you are fit for.'

I felt my ears redden. I had never in my

215

life been spoken to in that manner. I could have tipped the coffee over him, but it would hardly have helped my social calendar. I made coffees for all of us and handed them round carefully, not spilling a single drop. Pierre got his last.

'Glad you are feeling so much better,' I said. I longed for a handy jar of strychnine. Do they sell it in jars? 'We could do with an extra pair of hands.'

'Is that a snide remark about my illness?'

I was in no mood for an argument. The perfection of loathing would do instead. 'No way,' I barrelled on. 'We are so relieved to have you back at the helm. It was like a ship without a rudder.'

I don't think he liked that comparison, either.

14

Curaçao

We reached the Dutch Antilles through the last eddying gusts of the hurricane. The whole ship breathed a sigh of relief. The old inner hull tightened its grip on the new structure. Hurricane Ricky veered off out to sea, to batter new oceans and to terrify different dolphins.

Passengers came out of hibernation with tales of narrow escapes and miraculous acts of bravery and determination. Appetites returned, along with colourful deck clothes and the prospect of a day on land not far ahead. The aperitif of the day would sell in the hundreds. Curaçao Chaos, it was called. I have no idea what was in it.

'We can't wait to get on to terra firma,' passengers said, cruising the breakfast buffet for sustaining food. 'We've had enough of hurricanes to last a lifetime.'

We were late arriving at Willemstad,

Curaçao, but our berth at the new docks had been kept for us. Soon we had all lines fast and passengers could start going ashore. It was partly cloudy with occasional light showers. The right kind of weather for sightseeing.

The town of Willemstad was a pretty sight in the distance, with all the Dutch gables and pastel colours of the quayside buildings. There were two ways to cross the river, either by the Queen Wilhelmina Bridge or by free ferry. Although the passengers were on a cruise, they nearly all preferred to use the free ferry, to mingle with local people, dogs and babies, baskets of shopping. There was a fish market alongside the river's edge, produce of all kinds being sold from open boats bobbing on the water, and passengers flocked towards the photo opportunity. Their land legs were working again.

★ ★ ★

The previous day at sea had been a procedural nightmare and best submerged to the back of my mind. I had bitten on the bile and kept my composure. Pierre sharpened every warped barb in his repertoire and shot them straight at me. Most of them scored a hit, but I turned the other cheek every time. I would not be wounded or cowed by this monster.

If it had not been for my friends and colleagues, I might have broken down. But Debbie and Gary were brilliant, quietly supporting me, without causing more aggravation. They had their own work to do. Daniel Webster had some inkling of the situation. Word had spread round the observant crew. He caught me hurrying along a deck at a rate of knots in the worst weather.

'Hold on, Casey. Take it steady,' he said, taking my arm.

'I can't. I haven't time. Pierre expects me to work miracles.'

'Why has this odious man got it in for you?' he asked.

'It might be because I'm good at my job.'

'You won't be any good with a broken leg.'

Even Captain Wellington nodded in my direction on one of his routine deck tours. Nothing escaped him. He had eyes like a hawk.

Bruce was not slow to notice the inequality of assignments. He was following me through to the Cairo Lounge. I had the port lecture to do with slides. The current port lecturer was not well. Understandably not well. He'd taken to his bed with a stiff brandy.

'What's happened to coffee breaks, lunch breaks, cups of tea, normal sort of routine?' he asked, as I walked to my place on the stage and picked up the mike. I had an audience of fourteen stalwarts, each sitting in heavy armchairs, holding on to the arms. I was going to do a shortened version.

'I'm not allowed time to eat, drink, even go to the loo,' I said.

'Funny how I have suddenly discovered that I have to get an official statement from you about the state of Tracy Coleman's cabin. That's an order and it's urgent, if Pierre Arbour asks. You are an important witness. I'll see you in the

Boulevard Café in half an hour. Girl power. And don't be late.'

I flashed a quick smile of gratitude. 'Girl power.'

It was the only respite or cup of tea I had all day. Bruce had a tray with tea, a fruit scone, jam and cream ready on the table. I felt almost too sick to eat. But the tea was welcome. I drank two cups without stopping.

'Thank you, thank you,' I said. 'I haven't had a break all day. I've had more than everything to do as if it was a normal day at sea. I'm off to bingo next, then I have something else. A chocolate buffet? I don't remember what. I'd better go back to the office to check.'

'Hold on. You are doing nothing of the sort. You are staying here with me. I don't want a vital witness passing out on me.' Bruce sounded concerned. Perhaps he could see something desperate lurking in my eyes. I was trying to hide behind my normal composure. My clothes felt crumpled. I wanted to shower and change. I always put on a clean shirt in the afternoon.

'What about my statement?' I asked.

'That can wait. You had the foresight to have photos taken, and I've seen them. You enjoy your cup of tea and relax. Eat something, please. And tonight you are having supper with me.'

'Supper? You're joking. I very much doubt it,' I said, picking at some sultanas. The sweetness went straight to the back of my tongue. I could barely look at Bruce. I didn't want him to see me shredded like this. 'I'll be working non-stop. Pierre will think up something extra for me.'

And he did. I had both spectaculars to introduce to an audience of a dozen. They were hardly spectacular this evening. The celebrity pop trio did well in the circumstances, but they sat down instead of gyrating about the stage. The dancers did not even appear, on orders of the choreographer. Pierre took to his favourite bar for the evening, not up to anything more strenuous than bar propping.

One day I would get my moment of revenge. I was not usually a vengeful person, but I could not stop the mounting feeling.

★ ★ ★

Curaçao was a friendly place, with lots of culture and architectural heritage. It had also made a mass of money from the oil refineries built by Royal Dutch Shell in 1915, before they were closed in 1985. It was on the UNESCO World Heritage List and home to the oldest synagogue still in daily use. Today it was all tourism, offshore banking and ship repair.

It was one of my favourite places. The Arawak Indians inhabited it as far back as 6,000 years ago. They spoke a language called Papiamentu. The city had a deep natural harbour and that was worth more than all the gold, silver, spices or lumber being traded. It started trading sugar and salt and that was when the Jewish families from Amsterdam decided to settle.

The Dutch and Spanish Colonial-style houses lining the waterfront were perfect for strolling along or photographing. I loved the coral brick, the exact replicas of

Amsterdam, galleries with a series of arches and columns to extend buildings. It was all to provide shade from the searing Caribbean sun. One of the houses was called the Wedding Cake house. That's what it looked like, tiers of white arches.

I wondered if I would get any time off. Even a twenty-minute stroll along the open-air market towards the ferry point would be welcome.

No one had seen Pierre that morning. I was hoping he had died or been washed overboard. My normal sense of proportion or fairness had been completely lost during the previous day. It was the chain reaction to changes.

'So what shall we do?' I said to Debbie and Gary, who both looked washed out. 'Where is the master this morning?'

'Sleeping off a hangover, I expect,' said Gary wearily. 'He was drinking into the early hours. Liver damage on the horizon.'

'I've checked with tours. Almost everyone is going ashore today. They've had enough of the sea. We don't need any onboard activities. None at all.'

'So do we give ourselves the day off?' asked Gary.

'I really need a break,' said Debbie hopefully.

'We'll take turns,' I said, in charge again. 'You can either have the morning off or the afternoon off, but not both. That's fair, isn't it? If Pierre appears, then we can all go in front of the firing squad. I shan't wear a blindfold.'

So we sorted out shore leave amicably. I took the morning. I had to get away, to recharge my batteries. I had to shake off the shackles, find some even keel, give myself a wide berth from the ship. Daniel Webster had not phoned to have a quayside drink, as he said he would. Debbie and Gary both wanted to sunbathe on deck, then go ashore in the afternoon. It suited all of us. I changed into casual clothes, bringing my hat against the needles of sun.

I strolled through the new dock area, passed market stalls selling garments that wouldn't fit and souvenirs that you would hate when you got home. But as I got nearer the ferry point, the real atmosphere of Curaçao began to encroach on my heart. It was a beautiful island. Worth a holiday one day.

It was a tropical paradise, but one with a nucleus of civilization. It had art and literature, galleries and exhibitions, yet stunning beaches were only a taxi ride away. It had lush tropical gardens with exotic animals. All I wanted was a cool drink with Bruce Everton and a talk to sort out my mind.

Bruce caught up with me. We hung over the rail of the ferry for the three-minute journey for three minutes of bliss, not talking, listening to the lingo around us. I shrugged off the aggression of yesterday. I forgot Pierre, but I could not forget Tracy or Lorna.

Bruce helped me step ashore from the rocking ferry, and we went straight to the nearest quayside café. He ordered for me. All I wanted to do was soak in the fresh moments of freedom, the dappled sun on my face and a cooling breeze round my bare shoulders. I had a weakness for quayside cafés.

'I've ordered for you, is that all right?' he asked, leaning towards me over the glass-topped table. It had been wiped clean by a girl in the briefest denim shorts.

'Wonderful,' I said. 'I could drink anything.'

'You will like this. A speciality of the house.' Bruce was looking more relaxed this morning, although it's difficult to know what a relaxed detective looks like.

My drink arrived, a huge frothy milkshake in a tall glass. OK, a milkshake was fine, a healthy drink. Then I took my first taste. It was laced with the island's famous blue liqueur. Guaranteed to blow your mind, but delightful in sips. Bruce was drinking a cold beer. A plate of nibbles arrived. Dutch cheese, prune tarts, rum cake and *bolo di kashupete*, a butter cake covered in cashew frosting. And this was only elevenses.

'You're determined to fatten me up,' I said. 'Did you know that Curaçao liqueur comes from a recipe made by the Senior family in 1886 and it's still used? It's made from the Valencia orange which is so bitter when grown here that even the island goats won't eat it.'

'Goats have no taste.'

'But I think it's delicious.'

'A woman of beauty is a joy forever.'

'Is that a policeman talking?' I asked, nearly choking on my second mouthful of alcohol-laced froth. 'Or a lover-to-be?'

Bruce didn't answer straight away. He was disconcerted.

'Sorry,' I said. 'It's the alcohol talking.'

He had the grace to look embarrassed. 'I looked that one up. Someone said something like it. Not Oscar Wilde, but close. Sorry, Casey. You are beautiful, but you don't know it. And it's difficult for me to deal with. I'm used to corpses and mutilated bodies.'

'It was Keats, actually. A thing of beauty, etc.'

'Thank you.'

'But this is your time off, too,' I said, trying to bring the atmosphere back to normal and spiking a cube of soft local cheese. 'So we won't talk about your cases. We will talk about how to take revenge on Pierre Arbour, the entertainment director from hell. Nothing too damaging to my annual career review, but something essentially humiliating and totally satisfying to all and sundry who will witness said public humiliation.'

Bruce laughed, his brown eyes full of sympathy. 'I will give this my most earnest thought and let you know when I have a brilliant idea. Occasionally, I do have a brilliant idea and I assure you, it will be my first priority. But if I am to be honest with you, and I am always honest with you, it will be my third priority.'

I understood. He had two women in freezers who had priority. Bruce was relaxing in the calming atmosphere of the waterfront beside all the pastel-shaded houses with Dutch gables and pretty facades. He wore light-coloured trousers and an open-necked shirt. I was wearing a navy sundress with thin straps. My bare shoulders were lightly tanned, my hair loose. I spotted many of our passengers wandering around with cameras and videos, soaking up the tranquillity after the hurricane.

'You kissed me,' I said at last.

Bruce took a deep breath. 'I know. How could I ever forget?'

'Did it mean anything?' It was the liqueur talking again. 'I have to know.'

'Yes, it meant a lot, Casey. One day, when this is all over, when everything is over, we'll talk about it. Can you wait?'

So what did that mean? When what was all over? This case, his marriage, the cruise? I was no wiser. But I was wise enough not to press the matter. I gave him a liqueur-laced, eyelash-fluttering smile.

'I can wait,' I said. A second milkshake helped a lot. The tenseness went from the air. It was a morning of tangled thoughts.

We strolled around the town, not quite hand in hand, but almost, occasionally brushing hips. Cafés, restaurants, shops, bars, mansions and government buildings sprawled along every street. It was a honeymooner's paradise. A little train rattled round, filled with footsore tourists.

'You know, Casey, your help is often underestimated,' he said. 'You observe things overlooked by others and some-times the guilty fall through cracks in the system. You're able to cut corners and ask questions that the authorities can't do without officialdom behind them.'

'Short cuts?' I was still walking on alcoholic froth. It was idyllic.

'I'm relying on you to come up with some new leads. So far, I have nothing. The crew has clammed up on Tracy Coleman. The Russian pianist has retreated into a state of melancholy and refuses to see me. John Fletcher has nothing more to say about the state of his wife's mind, though he did admit to the quiz cheating. She was in contact with one of the ship's librarians. Dr Skinner is not exactly a forensic expert. And she has her hands full with patients injured during the hurricane.'

'Two are being flown home today.'

'That's sad.'

'They'll be offered a free cruise to make up for the disappointment.'

'But it's not the same, is it? And they have the pain and discomfort of some limb in plaster to put up with. And weeks to endure in an NHS hospital.'

'I also have a clue about the cleaning

fluid spilled in Pierre's cabin. Apparently, a few days earlier he had asked a steward for some to clean his camera equipment. Rather a coincidence.'

Speak of the devil. Out of the corner of my eye, I could see a white Panama hat tilted at an angle, slicked-back hair and the cut of an immaculate blazer. I would know that look anywhere. Pierre was going into the Royal Gems jewellers on Herenstraat, a posh jewellery shop. At his side was a woman that I recognized, too. He had his hand on her arm as he steered her inside.

15

At Sea

That evening, as he introduced the two shows, Pierre wore a flashy gold signet ring on his right hand. The diamond flashed in the stage light. It shone brighter than the dancers' rhinestone costumes. His white dinner jacket was sharp, too.

That night it was a Stephen Sondheim show, all his brilliantly satirical songs and poignant melodies. Pierre had not said a word about my organizing shore leave for our team. As far as I was concerned, the poor man had still been sick in bed, suffering. How was I to know that he was up and about and shopping? I did my best, as deputy, didn't I, in the circumstances?

We were set on an easterly course through the Caribbean Sea, towards the Venezuelan island of Isla Margarita.

Hurricane Ricky was a bad memory. The sky was half-cloudy and half-sunny. The perfect weather for lounging on deck with a bottle of suntan lotion.

I had been thinking about what Bruce had said, that what amateur sleuths do is get evidence that has been overlooked by others, then present it to the right authorities. Exposing the truth is what it is all about. Whether the case is solved or the right person charged with a criminal offence is not my business.

There was still a couple from the winning quiz team that I had not found or managed to speak to. Hurricane Ricky had thrown a Goliath-sized spanner into the works. Mr and Mrs Angus MacDonald were the missing pegs in the mystery of Lorna Fletcher's death.

They were avid bridge players. It took time to track them down and prise them out of the bridge room. They were a couple in their fifties, so well married to each other that they looked the same. Both had iron-grey hair in no-nonsense short styles. They wore identical clothes.

Grey shorts and white Aertex open-necked shirts or fawn trousers and red sweatshirts and sneakers. It was a uniform. In the evenings they both wore unrelieved black. Different shoes.

I caught them in the library, immersed in crime books. They liked puzzles. They looked at me as if they had never seen me before. They did not remember me as the quiz hostess. I had merely been a face with the answers.

'Have you a moment? May I talk to you?' I asked.

'Sshh,' they said in unison. 'No talking in the library.'

'Perhaps you'd like a drink in the bar?' I suggested.

The invitation did not need repeating. Their books closed in nanoseconds. They were up and out of their armchairs, following me to the nearby bar. Even though alcohol was cheap on board ship, perhaps they still had to be careful. Not everyone was a lottery winner or on a big bonus.

But their drink orders were modest, not taking me to the outer limits of alcohol consumption. I began to like them as I sipped my iced orange juice.

'I know we are all truly saddened by the unexpected death of Lorna Fletcher, and we still cannot believe that she is not with us. But I wondered if you could tell me a little more about her, what kind of person she was and if she said anything about being depressed in any way.'

'She certainly wasn't depressed,' said Angus MacDonald, an ordinary-looking, mediocre sort of person. 'She was on a high, enjoying the cruise, loving the quiz, especially winning every night. She'd been looking forward to this cruise.'

'Lorna loved the quiz. It was the highlight of her day,' added Mrs Mac-Donald. I learned later that her name was Fiona. 'Of course, we didn't know anything about the cheating. She thought that up and we've no idea why. We were a bright team without needing to cheat. That came as a real surprise to us. We would never cheat. We're bridge players.'

I smiled reassuringly. I believed them as much as I believed Big Ben struck thirteen occasionally. 'It was a great shock to all of us,' I agreed. 'We've never had a case of cheating before. The quiz is for fun and enjoyment. It doesn't actually matter who wins, as long as everyone has a good time.'

'Exactly,' said Angus MacDonald, finishing his drink. 'It's what we have always thought. It's not about the winning, although we never saw a single drop of the bottle of champagne.'

Fiona MacDonald laughed, disturbing her wrinkles. 'It always disappeared into their cabin.'

'Faster than you can say: it's all over, folks.'

'You mean, you never got any of the winnings despite being part of the team? They didn't open the bottle straight away and share it around?'

'You're joking. It vanished. Straight down to their cabin, I suppose.'

'Didn't this upset you?'

'Not really. We're not drinkers. We're more players.'

'Would you like some top-ups?' I asked.

They both nodded. A steward brought a dish of olives and a dish of carrot sticks and nuts. He was on my side and slipped a wink. I didn't know his name. I should find out.

'Tell me more,' I said, when the new drinks arrived. 'This is fascinating. I mean, I know nothing about the players who come regularly to the quiz. What else do you know about our regulars?'

'Gina is a prostitute.'

This was from Angus. It shocked even me. I quite liked her. Her silvery-blonde hair always looked sleek and she wore fairly smart clothes, nothing over the top. If she was a prostitute, then she was certainly a classy one. Even prostitutes need to take holidays, perhaps even more so, given their hours.

'She has approached almost every male passenger on board. She charges sixty pounds a half-hour, takes dollars, euros. Sometimes she does it for free, if you have the right face.'

'Ye Gods,' I said. I hadn't spotted that. Call me blind. I didn't ask him how he knew.

'So now you know,' said Fiona, spiking an olive with a stab.

'What can you do about it?' Angus asked.

'Not a lot unless someone makes a formal complaint. We can hardly turf her off at the next port. She might need a holiday.'

This conversation had thrown me. They say that conversation can be dangerous. And this one was reaching a danger zone. Time to backtrack.

'Let's get back to Lorna. What do you know about her as a person?'

'She loved quizzes and books. She hated her husband. John is a boring old soak, golf mad. She drank too much to make up for being left out.'

The woman was now in a freezer with all her secrets. I was beginning to feel sorry about asking all these questions, but somehow I still knew that she had not taken her own life. Lorna seemed much too vibrant and enthusiastic about life.

'How do you know this? Can you be sure?'

'Of course I'm sure,' said Fiona. 'I've known her all my life. She was my sister.'

＊　＊　＊

How little we know about our fellow travellers. So Fiona and Lorna were sisters. Once she had admitted their relationship, Fiona relaxed and began to tell me all about their family. And she began to munch her way through the olives and nuts.

'To be exact, we are half-sisters. Same mum, different dads. Our mother married twice. Her father was English, mine was a Scot, but we spent most of our childhood together. We went to the same school, holidays together, played together most of the time. We were even Girl Guides in the same troop.'

'Did you get the same badges?' I asked, before I could stop myself.

'No, she was the clever one. Morse code, first aid. I managed to scrape by with fire-lighting and hostess badges.'

'Useful,' I said.

'Then Lorna went to university to do economics and religious studies. I've no idea why she did religion. An easy option, perhaps. I went to secretarial college.

You'll never be without a job if you can type, my mother said.'

'That's true.'

'But those were mostly dead-end jobs, typing dull monthly reports, sales rep figures, standard letters to enquiries, the same thing over and over again. My boss used to say to me 'Standard letter number three, Fiona, then standard letter number four and alter the required quantity'. He wasn't needed, totally redundant. I could do it all standing on my head.' There was an element of frustration in her voice.

I tried to imagine years of typing standard letters, before the days of computers and simply clicking a print button.

'But you did meet me at one of those dead-end jobs,' said Angus wryly. 'Surely that wasn't so bad?'

She gave him a look that was difficult to fathom. There was a degree of affection in it, laced with tolerance and resignation.

'That was the only good thing that happened,' she had the grace to say.

'Lorna made a fortuitous marriage,' said Angus. 'She married someone who had a steady job and a decent pension. He also inherited money from his parents. I think this was their ninth cruise. I've lost count. Ask John. He can rattle them off. They always pretended to be hard-up, needing to save for the cruises.'

'So she had no need to cheat to win a bottle of champagne. They could buy as many bottles as they wanted?' I asked.

Fiona nodded. 'It was the thrill of cheating and not being found out. She probably went shoplifting in M&S, just for the thrill.'

'Did she know that I had spotted her?'

'She never said anything. I don't really know.'

'Surely she wouldn't have killed herself because of that?' I was suddenly over-whelmed with guilt, that perhaps I had been the cause of her death. 'No one kills themselves because they have been caught cheating.'

'How do we know what goes on in people's minds?' said Fiona, giving me a sharp look. 'You could have been the reason why she hung herself.'

I was getting out of my depth. It was not going the way I wanted. My conscience was fragile and I couldn't cope with anything extra, especially anything muddy. I stood up, holding on to the edge of the table. The ship was pitching to a different rhythm.

'No, I'm sure she was sensible enough to know that there would be no repercussions as long as she stopped. We are hardly a police regime. It's a fun quiz and we want everyone to have fun.'

I saw Bruce Everton hovering in the entrance to the bar. He looked at me and beckoned me with a slight movement of his head.

'Will you excuse me? Thank you for talking. My sympathy, Mrs MacDonald, for losing your sister. I didn't know.'

'Thank you. Nobody knew. Nobody else has said they are sorry.'

'Well, I'm sorry.'

I hurried away before I did anything I might be more sorry about. Bruce sensed that I was upset and steered me out of the bar, through the lounge and out on deck. We were being allowed on deck again. It was considered a bit rough, but safe enough.

'Good time or not a good time?'

'Not a good time for me, but a good time for you to talk to me,' I said. 'Treble Dutch, I know, but I need some straight-forward conversation.'

'Who were you talking to?'

'Angus and Fiona MacDonald, two of the winning quiz team that Lorna Fletcher belonged to. But I don't want to talk about it yet.'

Bruce Everton found a sheltered spot in the lee of a tender. The force-six wind cut around us, but it wasn't cold. This was the Caribbean. He was looking tired. He looked every one of his forty-nine years and a few extra.

'What's the matter?' I asked. 'You look tired.'

'That hurricane knocked the guts out of me. My legs are made for firmer land, Casey. I'm not a sea person, I've discovered. It is exhilarating, but only for short lengths of time. I'm surprised we're not at the bottom of the sea.'

Not a sea person. He was distancing himself from me. It was the second blow of the day. Here was I, nursing fragile thoughts about the detective chief inspector and myself, daydreaming of days together and maybe a few nights. I was not bothered by the age gap. It was not that intimidating. Close your eyes and he was young and virile again.

'Do you have to stay on board any longer, Casey? Can you get off soon and go home?'

'Barbados, maybe, if they get another replacement out to the ship by then. I'm only temporary. Why?'

'It's not safe, Casey. Those two deaths are linked. Tracy Coleman and Lorna Fletcher. I think you should go home as soon as you can.'

'What are you trying to tell me?'

'They were both murdered, and by the same person. It was the same method in both cases. Strangulation by a method called the Spanish windlass.'

'What's that?' I shivered. It sounded like torture.

'A loop of material or cord is placed round the victim's neck and tightened with a stick, turning it quickly. It's like a tourniquet. If the victim is taken by surprise and it's done quickly, then quite a weak person can do it. The murderer doesn't need a strong arm.'

'How do you know this?' I didn't really want to know.

'Dr Skinner made a further examination. There's a small bone in the throat called the hyoid bone. In both women, this bone was fractured. It's a sure sign of strangulation.'

'Poor souls. How dreadful. Perhaps they knew their killer, trusted them?'

'I think they did. There was no sign of a massive struggle. Then Lorna Fletcher was strung up to make it look like suicide. The murderer hoped Tracy wouldn't be found before he disposed of her body overboard. Hurricane Ricky was something he hadn't reckoned on.'

'You're saying he.'

Bruce shrugged. 'We always say he.'

'So why do you think I should go home as soon as possible?'

Bruce looked at me shrewdly. He was trying to decide whether to tell me or not. Sometimes I thought we could read each other's minds. He took my arm as if to shelter me from the bad news.

'Judith Skinner also found shreds of material under both victims' nails as if they had tried to tear off what was strangling them. And it was the same kind of material used to strangle both women.'

'And I'm not going to like this?'

'No, Casey, you're not. In both cases, it was a blue silk scarf like the one that you're wearing now as part of your uniform. I've seen you wearing one many times, tied round your neck.' Bruce paused. 'The murderer is someone who has access to your cabin or your clothes, or it's one of your female team.'

'Or someone who is trying to implicate the *Aveline* entertainment team.'

'Exactly.'

I slumped against him. 'It wasn't me,' I said. 'I didn't kill them.'

'I know, I know,' said Bruce. 'Don't worry. I'm not about to arrest you.'

'It was Tracy's own scarf,' I said, coming up for air. 'That makes sense, doesn't it? That's why her cabin was ransacked. We always carry spares. The murderer has a stock of them now.'

16

Isla Margarita

I'd been to the Venezuelan island of Isla Margarita many times and its cheerful, bustling pierside has never failed to cheer me. But not today. El Guamache was the only deep-water port in Margarita. The steel band was playing a welcome as fast as the three flag-wavers waved. The lines of stalls selling local wares were all ready to encourage passengers to leave their money behind on the island.

There were a variety of cafés and bars, sprucing up tables with flowers and putting on their smiles. There was one bar that did the most mouth-watering fruit punches, laced with something lethal. Pawpaw, mango, pineapple, whatever fruit you chose, the punch pumped alcohol straight to your veins.

I was not in the mood for escorting, so

I stayed on board and did my goodwill rounds of those passengers who also chose not to go ashore. It was the ideal place for wheelchair passengers, as everything was right there on the pierside and they did not have far to go for anything.

Even the two small beaches were only a walk away, but there were some rough steps to negotiate. The island had once been the centre of the pearl industry and few could resist buying some pearls from the vendors. I'd bought a tiny band of seven misshapen pearls on my last visit. They were all colours from black through cream and pink and white to the shiniest brassy brown. I'd felt sorry for them because they were not perfect enough to be made into jewellery.

It was a colourful island, and all the tours would enjoy their sightseeing, especially if they went to the national park La Restinga which had sea, beaches, mangroves, seabirds and flamingos.

The one drawback of the island was the lack of regular refuse collection. Piles of rubbish bags were growing by the roadsides and would soon form immovable walls, and some of the outer beaches were awash with plastic debris.

'Not going ashore?' It was Daniel Webster taking some well-deserved time off. He'd had little sleep during the hurricane. 'I know some decent little seafood restaurants.'

'If that's an invitation, it sounds lovely, thank you, but no.' I didn't remind him of his invitation yesterday that never materialized. 'I think I should stay and do my duty. Debbie will enjoy spending her money on trinkets and souvenirs. I may go ashore for twenty minutes in the late afternoon, simply for one of those delicious fruit punches.'

'Harry's Bar? The one with all the photos of filmstars tacked to the bamboo walls? Sinatra, Grant, Bogart? Terrific place.'

'I honestly don't remember.'

Daniel grinned. 'I'm not surprised. His fruit punches are particularly lethal, especially when drunk on an empty stomach. Have a sandwich first. See you later, Casey.' He swung away and down the gangway. He was in trim khaki shorts and an open-necked white shirt. His legs were brown and looked good.

Debbie was next to go ashore. She also wore shorts, but the skimpiest I'd ever seen, and a one-shoulder crop top that would give her a funny tan if she was not careful. She was swinging a big bag.

'Going swimming,' she said, patting her bag. 'Can't wait.'

'Keep walking past the two beaches where the bars are and everyone else stops,' I said. 'Then you'll find lots of little private coves with takamaka trees for shade and the bluest water lapping the sand. You'll find one where you can be alone. But give yourself plenty of time to get back to the ship. The sea is very shallow. You might walk further than you think.'

'Sounds idyllic,' said Debbie. 'I've got my suntan lotion, my hat and a bottle of water. I'll be OK.'

Even Judith Skinner was going ashore. She was almost unrecognizable in fairly suburban cut-off fawn trousers and a summery top. She was already wearing very dark glasses and a big hat, and she hadn't left the ship.

'I rarely go ashore, so I deserve this. My little lot are all recovering nicely,' she said. 'They are in good hands and won't miss me for a couple of hours. I fancy treating myself to a pearl necklace.'

'They reckon on getting twenty pearls out of every hundred oysters.'

'That's a lot of oysters to eat.'

'And somewhere there's a dress decorated with one hundred thousand pearls.'

'Not my style.'

'You won't know which necklace to chose. But don't buy at the first stall you see, however tempting a price they offer. Have a good look round first. Eventually, you'll be glad that you didn't buy the first necklace you saw.'

'You are a fount of useless information, Casey,' she said.

'Even the misshapen pearls can be lovely.'

'It's the same with human beings,' she said, going down the gangway.

I was also the object of commiseration

from everyone who knew me. Poor Casey, having to stay on board. But I had things to do and I wanted the ship to myself. Pierre sauntered off, immaculate in a white suit, his Panama hat tilted. He nodded in my direction, but didn't speak to me. He'd taken in that I was wearing the Conway uniform, therefore staying on the ship.

Edmund Morgan came and stood beside me. He looked morose and preoccupied.

'Not going ashore?' I asked.

'Boots won't let me in case there is another . . . er . . . unfortunate incident. Two mysterious deaths on one cruise is two too many, he says. As if my hanging around on deck is going to stop another woman from being strangled.'

I must have gone white.

'Sorry, Casey. Didn't mean to sound so callous. It just came out. But as I said, what can I do?'

'Your presence can be reassuring,' I said. 'Like a bobby on the street. People always feel safer if they see a policeman walking about.'

'Fat lot I could do to stop a murder,' he said.

The man needed a good shake and some sense pounded in to him. 'I'll tell you what we are going to do. Today you and I are going to comb the ship, talk to every crew member, bar steward, cabin steward, waiter, find out when they last saw Tracy Coleman or Lorna Fletcher.'

'That's a big order.' He was already dumbing it down. 'No time.'

'No, it isn't. Write every sighting or non-sighting down. Something will come out of it. We'll find out some little detail that will help Bruce Everton in his investigations.'

'What's a non-sighting?'

I stifled a sigh. 'When they should have been somewhere and weren't there.' He was no wiser. How did Edmund ever get this job? He must have pulled more than a few strings.

He cheered up fractionally. 'We'll do this together? You and me?'

'You and me, together,' I said, flashing a totally false come-hither smile. He fell for it and cheered up immensely. He saw lots of possibilities for accidental intimacy.

'Great,' he said. 'I'll go and get some notebooks.'

Notebooks. Good God, he was going to fight off a murderer with a notebook. He hurried away, a sort of spring in his step. The nearest the man could get to a spring.

'Not going ashore, Miss Jones?'

It was the hundredth time I'd been asked, but I had to be civil. This time it was Captain Luke Wellington himself. He was spruce in his white uniform. The gold braid always dazzled. I shook my head, gave him the smile I reserved for the captain. He seemed to like it, but he wasn't taken in. Much too sensible.

'Nor you, Sir?'

'Paperwork to catch up on. It's the only chance I ever get. When we are not going anywhere and safely parked.'

'Hurricane Ricky must have been a horrendous time for you and the crew.'

'It was a little stressful,' he said. 'But the original *Aveline* was a sturdy ship, and the new hull and stabilizers did a good job. Last thing we expected, though. It veered suddenly, moments after the last weather forecast. It took us all by surprise.'

'You and your crew did very well. It was quite frightening.'

'I know,' said Captain Wellington. 'Even I was alarmed at times, though I had every faith in the strength of the ship. They say you are safer in a ship than in a building during a hurricane. Quite an eventful cruise. Hope we don't have any problems with pirates.'

'Pirates? Are we likely to?'

He coughed to cover a chuckle. 'It was a sort of a joke, Miss Jones. I'm better at steering a ship than at making jokes.'

'That's a relief. It was a fairly feeble joke.'

'They used to have a lot of trouble with pirates around these seas. The Spanish treasure ships attracted the pirates, especially the ones laden with pearls. The Spanish built some forts on Margarita, a star-shaped one at Pampatar and one at La Asuncion. You can still see them today.'

'At least we are not laden with pearls.'

'Some of our female passengers are laden with the equivalent. There's a lot of jewellery flashed around at the captain's cocktail parties. Sometimes I need dark glasses. Nice talking to you, Miss Jones. Have an easy day.'

He did a mild sort of salute, hand almost to cap, and walked away, doing his morning rounds before catching up with his paperwork. I hoped he'd have an easy day, too. The sun was rolling over in bales of heat.

Our clean sweep of crew and hotel staff, cabin stewards and entertainers took several hours, and also took a toll on our voices. I grew quite hoarse. Edmund was flagging. He hadn't worked so hard for days. Weeks, probably. We both needed frequent drinks and breaks. My back was starting to ache, and I hadn't had backache for years.

Edmund threw himself down on a chair on deck and flipped open his notebook. 'I can't make any sense of this,' he said. 'No one seems to have seen Tracy at all that day. She must have gone ashore.'

'We know where she was. She was with

the Russian pianist. But someone must have seen her before she went to his cabin, and later when she left. Romanoff says that she did leave him about four in the afternoon.'

'Then she could have gone ashore.'

'But she didn't. Her swipe card wasn't used.' The words fell from my mouth without thought. I'd been saying the same thing all day. Edmund didn't listen. 'We need to find out where she went to after leaving Romanoff. She must have been somewhere between then and her death.'

'No one seems to know,' he said morosely.

'Someone must know. She didn't suddenly become invisible and flit around the decks like Blithe Spirit.'

'Like who?'

'It's a character in a play.'

'And that Mrs Fletcher. No one seems to have seen her, either. Did she only emerge from her cabin for the quiz? She must have done something else.'

'I checked at the beauty salon, and she never had her hair or nails done. She always looked very smart. I suppose she did it herself in the cabin. The librarian brought her a selection of books, mostly novels.'

Passengers circulated around the cafeteria, bars and lounges. And, of course, the decks. Passengers were creatures of habit. They tended to have favourite places on deck and made a beeline for what they saw as their spot every day. John Fletcher had his spot on deck. It was sheltered and private, but no one ever saw his wife join him on deck.

'It was as if they weren't together. Mr and Mrs Fletcher shared a cabin and appeared in the dining room together, but for the rest of the day, they were living totally separate lives.'

'Except for the quiz,' Edmund added.

'Yes, except for the quiz.'

'Funny way to enjoy a cruise.'

'Doesn't this all seem very fishy to you, Edmund?'

'Fishy? I don't know what you mean.'

'Both women were travelling on the same ship. Both women keeping a very low profile. Then both women die, within days of each other,' I said. 'There has to be a connection.'

'Well, if you say so.'

'Think about it.' I stood up and smoothed down my rumpled skirt. Passengers were starting to return to the ship. I planned to stand at the head of the gangway and see if there was anyone who might be able to give me helpful information. There was a spare minute to tidy up in a washroom. My hair was veering towards nest status. No birds in sight.

'Why is there a blue band painted on all the trees, Casey?' a woman asked me as her purchases went through the scanning machine.

'The paint deters the ants. It stops them climbing up. Did you see the frigate birds and the pelicans?'

'And all the wild dogs in the rocks.'

Everyone seemed to have enjoyed their tours. They returned in good spirits, ready for showers, an excellent meal and even more spectacular entertainment — though I doubted if I would be introducing the shows tonight. But I would still wear a smashing dress. I'd brought them to wear, not simply to hang on a hanger.

An elderly man came slowly up the gangway, holding on to the rail with one hand, and using a walking stick with the other. He looked hot and tired. I didn't recognize him. Somehow I hadn't seen him before. He was one of the many who merged into the crowd.

'Have you had a good day?' I asked. 'Ready for a good meal and tonight's show?'

'I don't think so, Miss. My bed calls me.'

'That's a shame,' I said. 'It's a really excellent show tonight.'

'I'm sure it is, but I prefer a bottle of firewater brandy and an old film in my cabin. Not one for mixing.'

I felt sorry for him. Cruising is a lot about mixing, but he seemed to be a loner.

'Enjoy your film,' I said as he went through the security check. His carrier bag went through the scanning machine. It clinked.

He nodded and headed straight towards the nearest lift, his back bowed. He seemed to need help, but there wasn't a lot I could do. It was his choice to spend the cruise on his own. A sad choice.

I went over to the officer swiping the cruise cards in the machine. 'Who was that?' I asked. 'That elderly gentleman with a stick?'

'That was Henry Fellows,' replied the officer. 'Stocking up for another bender.'

★　★　★

I was talking to another passenger, my mind still full of sympathy for the old gentleman, when suddenly someone grasped my arm and swung me round. I nearly fell from the suddenness of the jerk. I came face to face with Fiona MacDonald. Her mouth was tight, her face contorted with fury.

'How dare you?' she hissed. 'How dare you go around asking everyone about my sister?'

I couldn't stop watching her mouth. I half-expected a serpent's tongue to suddenly dart out. It was time to duck.

'Please let go of my arm, Mrs MacDonald. I'm sorry if I have offended you in any way. Let's go and talk somewhere quieter.'

'You leave her alone!' she shouted. 'I won't allow it.'

'I'm sure there's some misunderstanding. I was trying to discover the truth about her death. It seemed very strange that no one ever saw her around the ship, only at dinner and the quiz nights.'

Fiona was trying to contain her rage. I couldn't understand why she was so angry with me.

'I'll tell you why no one ever saw Lorna around the ship. Because she couldn't stand people. She had a phobia. She couldn't stand crowds of people or big places. It came on slowly, menopausal. She had an irrational fear of crowds and open spaces. She suffered from agoraphobia.'

'I didn't know . . . ' I began.

'That's why we always had the table in the corner, in the alcove, well away from everyone. And you spoiled it all. You good as murdered her. You murdered my little sister.'

17

Mayreau

Throughout the early hours, the *Aveline* passed north of the islands of Grenada and Carriacou. We were on our way to the private island of Mayreau, a small, unspoiled and practically unreachable sandy outcrop of rock.

We had to anchor far out to sea and let the port anchor hold us to the seabed. Passengers would go ashore on the tenders. But, for once, there were no tours or trips or coaches waiting on the shore. The only organized trips were by schooner or catamaran, motorboat or glass-bottomed boat. The castaway tour sounded perfect, with a delicious lobster lunch on an island no bigger than a football pitch with sugar-white sand and warm blue sea. It even had a name. Morpion Island.

There was a single, perilously steep road

that went up to the village of Mayreau on the top of the hill. It was a hard, sweaty walk in the sun. But a couple of enterprising taxis would run passengers up the two-minute journey for ten dollars.

The drivers were on their way towards making a healthy bank balance, island size. Only those with good legs and good lungs actually managed the one-in-four climb to the village. The climb required lots of stops to enjoy the spectacular sea view and to catch your breath.

And when you got there, the village consisted of two roads. It had a diminutive church with a conical wooden roof right at the top of the hill and a small single-storied school. There was the usual scattering of local bars, a few shops and one enterprising hotel called Dennis's Hideaway, advertising a pint-sized pool.

I was there, enjoying the island, all because of Pierre.

★ ★ ★

I hoped I had earned a few hours ashore as I had been on duty all of yesterday and half the night. But Pierre thought otherwise. I was working at a computer when he stormed into the office.

'I understand you spent most of yesterday wandering round the ship making totally unnecessary enquiries and upsetting the passengers,' he said, flinging some papers onto the desk, his face set in grim lines.

'I beg your pardon?'

'You were supposed to be running activities and keeping the passengers occupied. Instead, you did your own thing, without my permission, and were intrusive and objectionable.'

I wasn't standing for this. So I stood up.

'Firstly, it is none of your business what I was doing and I didn't need your permission. Secondly, I had organized activities for the handful of passengers left on board, but most of them preferred to be left alone, to read, sunbathe, drink or play bridge.'

'Your usual excuses.'

'And who of the passengers complained and said I was being intrusive? I'd like names, please. And I'd like to see the written complaint.'

'There's not an actual written complaint. It was a verbal complaint. To me personally.'

'By whom?'

'I'm not at liberty to tell you.'

'For heaven's sake, Pierre, don't act like a complete idiot. If I am being reprimanded about some complaint, then I'm entitled to know who complained and what was said.' I could feel my temper rising and I rarely lose my temper.

'I find this attitude unacceptable, Casey.' He went to the coffee percolator and poured himself a cup. He didn't offer me one. Just as well. I might have thrown it over him, again. 'You were sent out here to me as a replacement of the highest category. I find this difficult to believe.'

And I found it difficult to believe this was happening. The man was impossible. Suddenly, the funny side struck me and it was beyond me to smother a smile.

'You can't mean this,' I said with a laugh, hardly knowing where to look or how to contain my amusement. Pierre sounded so pompous and ridiculous. He also looked pompous and ridiculous. 'I've done nothing wrong. Tracy Coleman was one of our team, our staff, and a valued colleague. Of course, we all want to find out what really happened.'

'Not at the expense of your proper duties. I'm grounding you, Casey, for the duration of your contract on the *Aveline*.' Then he realized the use of that phrase was hardly appropriate on board ship. 'I mean, I am confining you to your cabin.'

I shouldn't have laughed. That had been the final insult.

'You can't do this.'

'I certainly can.'

'Are you sure? OK, I'll go,' I said agreeably, foreseeing freedom. 'Do you want me to go now, or shall I finish putting together tomorrow's programme?'

Pierre had not thought through the consequences of one less pair of hands, one less pair of legs to run about. He'd have to do some work for a change. I could see his mind wondering how he could get out of this one.

'You will continue all office duties,

under supervision,' he said, his brain working in lightning flashes. 'But you will have no further contact with passengers. Do you understand? Finish tomorrow's programme now, by all means.' He closed his speech with a hostile grunt.

As soon as he had stalked out of the office, not having done a stroke of work, I emailed Head Office in London with a résumé of events. I was fair. I told them exactly what I had been doing and the current state of events. I also told them that I had a written permit from Captain Wellington which entitled me to go wherever I pleased on the ship.

They replied almost immediately, probably after holding a quick internal conference in the next room. I blessed my good relations with the office staff.

'Stay cool, Casey,' they emailed back. 'Pierre Arbour can't confine you to your cabin on such flimsy grounds. You would have to have done something really criminal or against company rules. We asked you to make these enquiries about Tracy Coleman. Do what you have to do to keep him quiet, then take the rest of the time off. Enjoy.'

And I would. I'd always wanted to stroll round a private Caribbean island, no commercialism, somewhere natural and peaceful. I might even get in a swim. With such enticing thoughts in mind, I got through the programme details at a rate of nautical knots.

I answered all current email enquiries, took some phone calls, solved a few trivial problems, did a quick tidy-up round the office, then left.

I put a note on Pierre's desk. 'Gone to my cabin. Shall lock myself in.'

Fat chance.

★   ★   ★

I went ashore on the next tender, wearing a swimsuit under a sarong and T-shirt. I knew how quickly one could burn under this hot sun. Lashings of factor 30 before and after a swim. But first I wanted to have a quick look round.

I'd always imagined a private Caribbean island to be flat with curving sandy beaches and dotted with palm trees. This one was a hill, a mound. A very steep hill surrounded by scattered beaches and trees sweeping down to the shore.

The ship's tender tied up at a short landing stage that was only wide enough for single file. It had been a rough ride and there were complaints. Someone mentioned an ebb tide.

Commercialism hit us straight away, but it was only the female villagers who had strung up lines between the trees and were displaying a selection of colourful T-shirts, sarongs and beach towels. Not much else.

It was a ramshackle place but with a certain charm. The locals were not used to cruise ships the size of an apartment block anchoring out at sea. We were eccentric strangers, an alien breed, something to gawp at. The children kept touching me, wanting to look at my hands, my feet, my clothes. They thought my hair was funny with its blonde streak.

I walked up the four-in-one unmade road while I still had the strength. The hot sun was sapping my energy. Dennis's Hideaway looked like a real hideaway place; no one would ever find you there. The seafood bar was called Robert Righteous and de Youths. Every wall was covered in decorations of a hundred different styles, and the food sounded delicious. 'All fish caught today', said the chalked menu board. I might well stay.

The church with the conical wooden roof was coldly dark inside. I sat on a tiny wooden pew and tried to say a prayer to someone about the state of the world. This island was a prayerful place. Outside the church, I tried my mobile phone, but it wouldn't work. Too far away from any masts to get a signal.

Children's voices lured me on still upward towards the school, on to the highest point. A fresh wind cooled me.

'Miss!'

'Miss!'

Children of all ages swarmed around on the playground, trim in shorts and T-shirts of different colours. The different colours showed which class they were in. There were about forty children aged from four to twelve.

'You from ship?'

'What's your name?'

'How old are you?'

'What is name of ship?'

They wanted to know everything. We were an event in their lives. The ship was an event. The passengers were live entertainment.

I had thought to arm myself with a stack of picture postcards of the ship, and I handed them out to a sea of eager hands. The children loved them. They were a gift, a souvenir. They were free.

I had my notebook, as always. The children wanted to sign it. There was Ronessa Hemson, who was nine. She put her age in brackets. Another nine-year-old called Tiffany Farde, and another Tiffany Ralph, who was ten. Tiffany was a popular name, it seemed. There were dozens of Tiffanys.

The school had three classrooms, all under one roof, the space divided by long blackboards. The children worked in chalk, and their handwriting was perfect, joined up, legible. They were a credit to their headteacher, Julian Ollivierre.

I could have stayed there. I wanted to

live and work here, teach something useful: English, maths, how to run cruise-ship entertainment. It was a wrench to drag myself away. But it would be a disaster to miss the ship. And I desperately wanted that promised swim.

The children stood waving until I was out of sight. It was easier walking downhill, but not without holding on to any shrub or bush within reach. And to think that the women of the village did this climb several times a day. They must have strong legs.

'Hi there, Miss Jones. Come and have a drink.'

It was Gina in that fringed gold bikini that left nothing to the imagination. She was propping up the beach bar, a large fruit punch of some kind in her hand. She came swaying over to me, bare feet kicking up sand, her lipstick smudged from too much drinking.

'Did I land you in it?' she asked.

I didn't know what she was talking about and then it clicked. 'You mean, with Pierre?' I asked, innocently.

'Yes,' she said, sucking the lethal brew

through a straw. 'I'm really sorry. It was only a silly remark. I didn't mean anything by it. He's such a prick, that man. But it hurt his pride and I suppose he took it out on you.'

'Only a standard reprimand,' I said. 'What did you say to him?'

'That you were a busy little bee. Flitting here and everywhere with your little notebook. Talking to everyone about Lorna Fletcher and Tracy Coleman.'

'No, he didn't like it, but I have broad shoulders and a kind heart. Don't you worry, Gina. My little notebook is bursting with interesting facts. But your secret is safe with us. Whatever you choose to do in your spare time is your business, offering free-range sex, maybe, and as long as it doesn't break any company rules, then we have to turn a blind eye.'

She went white under her melting colourfast tan, brushed on out of a bottle. She didn't know where to look. We were standing under a big-leafed tree where the leaves looked like dinner plates. There were nuts growing on it. The birds loved the nuts. They were swinging on the branches, pecking at their supper. I wished I had brought a camera.

'I don't know what you mean,' she spluttered. 'What do you want from me? I've already bought Pierre a ring.'

'Don't worry. I don't want anything from you. You don't have to buy me a ring. But don't tread on my toes.'

I wanted that swim more than I wanted to watch Gina suffer. The lapping waves were almost at my toe-tips. I shed the sarong and the T-shirt and in moments was swimming in cool crystal clear water, out of Gina's sight. The seabed was steeply shelving. I took my landline on a yellow hut. Made sure it was always in sight. I could be out of my depth in two strokes.

I swam for about ten delicious minutes, letting the water lap over me, eyes closed to the sun but always watching the yellow hut and refracted sunlight. Always checking the number of tenders ferrying passengers back to the ship. I had to be back on board and locked in my cabin before Pierre found out that I had been ashore.

I wondered how I would spend the evening. Watching in-cabin television? Replays of *Dad's Army*? Pierre would be introducing the show tonight. A winning TV girl pop group had joined the ship at Panama City, but they had been laid low with sea sickness almost from the start. Tonight they were doing their first show. He would not miss the opportunity of going on stage with the bevy of beauties, orchestrating the applause.

I felt sad leaving the tiny island. But it was only a dream. The tender took us back to our floating village. I was still damp under my sarong.

I could eat when Pierre was on stage. I'd sneak up to the Boulevard Café, heavily disguised, eat and grab myself as much food as I could carry. I'd be like a tracksuited camel. I'd fill my pockets.

Once everyone was back on board ship and all the pre-departure checks had been made, I heard the port anchor being heaved up. It was a late departure, as one of the schooners had returned well after its stipulated time due to a heavy swell. It had been an ambitious seven-hour trip to the Grenadine Islands, including a beach lunch and lots of swimming and snorkelling. We were leaving the bay of Mayreau and heading west then north towards St Lucia.

As soon as I was sure that Pierre was busy introducing the girl group, I hurried up to the Boulevard Café in the lift. My tray looked as if I was stocking up for a siege, as I was. I stockpiled apples, bananas, cheese, packets of biscuits, anything that was easy to carry and unsquashable. But I stopped long enough for a plate of ribbon pasta with a delicious mushroom and feta cheese sauce and some fruit salad. That meal would have to last me a long time.

I took my tray of spoils down to my cabin. It was not generally allowed to remove food from the café, but the stewards did not seemed to notice. Or they pretended not to. I could be taking the food to a sick friend.

It was dark now and the sea lapped against my cabin window. I sat down to write up my notes for the day, including my encounter with Gina. My music centre was playing a favourite Gershwin piano concerto.

A strange noise seemed to be coming from somewhere above, and I could not recognize the sound. It sounded like vague shouting and screams. An object fell past my window and into the sea. It was a deck chair. I could not believe what I had seen. I turned off the music and peered through the glass.

A second deck chair fell into the sea. Then came a small drinks table. This was ridiculous. Had the passengers rioted on deck? Was the dinner menu below standard?

As I turned to leave my cabin and investigate, a dark shape loomed against the glass of my cabin window. It was the bow of a small vessel, a speedboat of some sort, rocking on the waves, close to our ship's hull. It was so near, I could have almost touched it.

Suddenly, I heard gunshots. The gunfire was exploding into the night air. It was unbelievable. I knew instantly what was happening. Our ship was being boarded by pirates.

18

At Sea

I could see that the pirates were armed with Kalashnikovs and wearing fawn camouflage gear and masks. They were trying to board the *Countess Aveline* with grappling hooks and ladders, but the passengers were not having their idyllic cruise interrupted by a crowd of raiders. They were hurling tables and chairs over the side of the ship and onto the heads of the invaders.

'Get off! Go away!' they shouted with a variety of olde English oaths. All these nicely mannered people had suddenly become quite ferocious.

Captain Wellington was making an announcement over the tannoy. I could hear his voice as I hurried on deck. There was chaos everywhere. Passengers were running about, some videoing the incident, others continuing to throw deck furniture overboard. I saw one woman taking aim with her shoes — a real sacrifice if they were Jimmy Choo or Christian Louboutin.

'I advise all passengers to go back to their cabins and to lock themselves in. I can assure you that the crew can deal with this unfortunate incident. Please leave the decks. Please leave the decks immediately. This is for your own safety.'

He underlined the word immediately with a stern tone.

'They're shooting at us. We can hear bullets clanging as they hit the ship,' said a woman, grabbing my arm. 'It's awful. What shall I do?'

'Go to your cabin and lock yourself in,' I said. 'We have security guards who can deal with this.'

Brave words. I doubted if our security officer could do anything. But I realized that the captain had emergency measures. Perhaps he had specially trained crew at the ready. There had been other incidents of pirates boarding cruise ships, particularly in the Indian Ocean. Rich pickings could be found among the passengers: jewellery, credit cards, passports, as well as the vast amount of cash and currency carried on board.

There was little I could do, except reassure passengers and persuade them to go back to their cabins.

Two of the pirates were climbing over the rail, having evaded the flying deck chairs, tables, and stilettos. They had begun peppering the deck with bullets. Small beads of fear trickled along my spine as I backed off. I didn't want to get shot.

Suddenly, the deck was plunged into darkness as the gunfire took out the lights. There was an outcry of confusion as passengers tried to reach the doors to the decks. The cover of darkness was what the raiders wanted. I could hear their voices as they shouted to each other in a language I did not recognize.

More raiders climbed onto the deck, having apparently fixed a ladder. My eyes quickly became accustomed to the darkness, and I was able to guide passengers to the heavy doors. Many clung to my arm as if I were some sort of safe talisman.

'Help me, help me. I can't see.'

Then the emergency lights came on, and the raiders rushed to the doors to block their use. They tried to herd the remaining passengers to the back of the deck so they could go through their handbags and pockets and take their jewellery. The pirates would keep them out of their cabins and then make a search of the cabins for more goods. The key cards weren't marked, so the pirates would have to batter down the doors. They were carrying axes. One of them ripped a gold necklace from a woman's throat, and she cried out in pain and indignation.

Members of the crew appeared out of nowhere, firing into the air with pistols and spraying the attackers with the firehoses. The streams of water were more effective than the pistols, which I guessed were only firing blanks. Commercial ships are not allowed to carry weapons, although I had heard of some Italian lines hiring their own armed security guards.

Now the decks were slippery with water. Several passengers slipped and fell in their haste to get below.

'My dress is ruined. Look at it,' said one woman as I helped her to her feet and guided her to a door. 'I'll never be able to replace it.'

'Better a ruined dress than losing all those beautiful rings you are wearing,' I said. I didn't mention the diamonds flashing in her ears. They would have been torn out in a second.

One of the raiders bumped right into me, the butt of his gun digging into my ribs. His eyes glinted behind his mask. But the interest was only momentary. I didn't look much of a catch in my tracksuit and tight head scarf, pockets bulging with apples and biscuits.

'Servant, maid, domestic,' I gabbled, saying any word I could think of in the lowly status. '*Domestico. Femme de chambre. Servizio. Donna delle pulizie. Lavandería.* Worker.' I did a sort of ironing pantomime. He seemed to understand and pushed me away. I drew a deep breath.

Some of the stranded passengers had not been so lucky. They were being herded in to the pool area and were being searched for jewellery and other valuables. Several women were crying, their partners watching helplessly.

'Down, down, down!' they shouted, forcing everyone to lay down on the wet decking. Some of the elderly ladies found this too difficult and clung to the rails.

Gina was hysterical as they ripped off her necklace, earrings, bracelet and diamond watch. Her face was quivering with rage. 'They are not real!' she screamed. 'They are all imitation, you fools. Fakes. Artificial. You're wasting your time.'

The crew was valiantly trying to dodge the gunfire and aim their hoses at the same time. Everyone was getting wet. The noise was horrendous, with the raiders screaming and shouting in a language that no one understood. Perhaps it was as well that we didn't.

There were only a handful of them, maybe six or eight, but it was difficult to tell when they were all over the place. But they had lethal guns, and the last thing anyone wanted were injuries and real casualties.

One of the heavy doors flung open, and some idiot actually flounced out on the deck, striding into the melee with indignation and wrath.

'What the hell is going on?' he shouted. 'Don't you know that you are ruining an absolutely brilliant show with all this ridiculous noise?'

It was Pierre, in his white dinner jacket and trousers, flamboyant red bow tie and cummerbund. His new ring flashed and sparkled as he waved his arms at the raiders.

I could not believe that the man didn't see what was going on.

'I demand that you stop this noise at once!' he shouted, trying to make himself heard. His Rolex caught the eye of a couple of raiders. 'I am in charge here, and you are asking for trouble.'

Instantly, they were on him. They dragged him to the side of the deck. The ring and watch were off and tossed into bags.

I didn't understand why they did not let him go at that. Instead, they bundled him into a corner and began tying his ankles and his arms behind his back. In moments, he was as trussed as a chicken.

They must have thought he was the captain. It was the voice of command, the attitude, the posture. The captain's voice had only been a sound over the tannoy. They had no way of knowing that the real captain was still very much in charge on the bridge.

I felt sorry for Pierre for all of five seconds. His beautiful white suit was being ruined.

'Hostage man! Man hostage!' shouted the raider who seemed to be in charge. He was waving his Kalashnikov. 'You give much money for man. We kill.'

'Can't you do something to help?' Gina asked me. She had managed to get away in the darkness but was upset and dishevelled. She was rubbing her wrists. 'He's your boss. You're the deputy.'

It said nothing in my job description

about rescuing the entertainments director from pirates. Unless it was in the
small print.

'I think it would only make matters
worse if I interfered,' I said. 'This is one
situation we are not trained for. Besides, I
don't know what I could do.'

'I've got a gun,' she said. 'Do you want
it?'

She said it in a matter-of-fact voice as if
she were offering to lend me her mascara.
I blinked rapidly.

'You've got a gun? Is it loaded?'

'Yes, sometimes I have . . . er, clients
who become rather difficult. A gun soon
sorts things out.'

I doubted if it would sort this out. I
had never fired one, not even at a fun fair
to win a teddy bear.

'Where is it?' I asked.

'Tucked in my bra.'

'How did you get it on board?'

'You do ask a lot of questions, young
lady. Do you want it or not?'

They had dragged Pierre under a
spotlight. He looked dreadful, all dignity
gone, suit ruined. There was a gag in his

mouth, some dirty bit of cloth tied round his face.

'Yes,' I said, making up my mind. I had no idea what I was going to do or why I should rescue Pierre Arbour. He had been nothing but a pain in the rear.

'I'll slide behind this lifeboat and retrieve it for you. Where are you going to keep it?' Gina sounded cheered, as if she was an extra in a movie.

'Same place,' I said.

★   ★   ★

The gun was cold against my skin. The shape of the gun gave me a funny-looking bustline but who was noticing in this situation? I wondered where Bruce Everton was and what he was doing. Surely he was the man to take charge? Surely he had dealt with hostage situations before?

Perhaps he was contacting some friendly naval base, asking for reinforcements. A couple of frigates might, at this instance, be speeding towards us, armed to the hilt.

'Money, money, give us lots of money!' the leader shrieked, waving his gun about. 'We kill.'

And where was Edmund? In his office, drawing up some contingency plan, a basic get-out strategy in case of some unforeseen event?

A tracksuit did not seem the right gear for confronting these determined raiders, who were rapidly relieving our passengers of their worldly goods. But something had to be done fast for their sakes. There were faces I knew well, and they looked pale and distraught.

On the other side of the door I caught a glimpse of a cabin steward's trolley. The steward must have been servicing the two luxury penthouse suites on this deck. On the carpeted floor lay a drawstring linen bag for dirty laundry. In seconds I darted in and took the bag.

I slung the bag over my shoulder and marched determinedly forward, pushing through the crowd to where the raiders were busy emptying handbags onto the deck. Lipsticks rolled in all directions, lace hankies were trodden into puddles.

'Stop!' I said loudly in my most commanding voice. Lots of stage voice projection. 'Stop this at once. I have the money for the hostage.'

'Money?' The leader slid forward out of the crowd. I couldn't see much of him, only his eyes. 'Much money?'

'A lot of money. Stop,' I said again. 'Stay where you are.' I thrust my hand out, palm forward. I had no intention of handing him the bag until Pierre was returned, in whatever shape he was now in. 'Don't move.'

'Nice lady, give money now!' he shouted, still moving forward.

I dropped the bag at my feet, whipped out the gun and held it two-handed, pointing it straight at him, with my feet apart, best television lady cop style. It was a small automatic with a pearl handle. I had no idea if the safety catch was on or off, nor did I have any idea how to release it.

'No. Man first, money after.' My English was rapidly descending to his level. He would not stop moving towards me. It was scary, and my mouth had gone dry. Several of the passengers had retreated, and the other raiders seemed to have become frozen. Maybe a domestic toting a gun was a novelty.

'Money now!' he shrieked.

I hadn't intended to do it. A sort of unconscious reflex action took over. I stepped back and pulled the trigger, aiming not at him, but at the laundry bag. There was a sharp explosion, and bits of bag flew in all directions. It was obvious that a real bullet had been fired.

'You next!' I shouted, aiming directly at the leader.

He stopped.

It was at that moment that Captain Wellington came to the rescue. From all sides, crew poured onto the deck, armed with batons, safety nets and various heavy implements. The raiders took one look at the armed crew and leaped over the side, tumbling down their ladders to their speedboat, some of them still firing indiscriminately. Seamen hacked at the ladders attached to the side of the ship and they fell away. The speedboat's engine began revving. One raider was caught in a safety net and pinioned down. Unfortunately, Pierre was also caught, sprawled, in a net. It was not one of his best evenings.

I was trembling, the gun still in my hand. Bruce Everton was hurrying through the crowd towards me, thrusting people aside. He was in his shirtsleeves, face grim and serious.

'Casey,' he said. 'Are you all right? You were brilliant. But it was very stupid to pull a trick like that. Anything could have happened. You could have been shot.'

I nodded in agreement.

'We knew what we were doing, but certainly you gave us the opportunity to catch them by surprise. The captain wants to thank you.'

'Does he?'

'Now give me the gun.'

I was holding my arm against my side. Bruce took the gun out of my stiff fingers. Then he noticed the blood oozing from between the fingers at my side.

'I think I have been shot,' I said.

Then I fainted.

19

At Sea

It would have been lovely to record that I fainted daintily into Bruce's arms but I missed. I actually fainted onto the laundry bag. My last thought as I smelled a whiff of cordite was, would the hotel manager charge me for the ruined pillowcases?

One raider had been using a small-bore sawn-off shotgun, and the wound in my arm was made by a lead pellet, they told me later. It could have been worse. It had entered the fleshy part of my arm, leaving an abrasion ring and scorching.

I refused a stretcher, but they insisted on wheeling me down to the medical centre. Passengers cheered and clapped. Down among the casualties, all I wanted was a hot drink — preferably a strong coffee, no sugar.

'Only water,' said Judith Skinner,

ruthlessly cutting away the sleeve of my favourite tracksuit. She was not a bit like Dr Samuel Mallory. He would have tried to save the garment. 'In case I have to get the pellet out under an anaesthetic.'

'Dig it out,' I said, gritting my teeth. But she had already put a local injection into my arm and the area was going numb. She extracted the pellet with forceps and dropped it into a kidney tray. It made a clinking noise.

'There's a souvenir for you. Helen will put it in an envelope.'

'I'll have it mounted.'

'Didn't touch the bone, thank goodness,' she went on. 'It could have been nasty. A nice clean wound.'

'Hardly felt it,' I murmured.

'Too busy being a heroine,' she said.

'I think Casey deserves a cup of tea,' said Bruce. He had been at my side all through the procedure, giving silent moral support. 'After what she's been through.'

'Water,' said Dr Skinner. She'd fixed a saline drip into my other arm, so there was no way I could have held a cup. A nurse held some water to my lips. Try drinking when someone else holds the cup. My mouth seemed to be in the wrong place. It dribbled down my chin.

'How about something stronger for Casey? Surely you have some medicinal brandy? I could order champagne?'

'First things first. And if you continue to annoy me, Chief Inspector, I shall have to ask you to leave the medical centre.'

She was a real Boudicca without the horses or the whip.

The medical centre was full. There were quite a few casualties, mainly passengers who had fallen on the wet decks or were in shock over the whole episode. Many were elderly with weak hearts. I was the only person who'd been shot, and as staff, I suppose I didn't really count.

'I'm OK now,' I said. 'A couple of paracetamols and a plaster, and I can go.'

'You're not going anywhere,' said Judith. 'You need stitching up and a decent sleep. And I've just the bed for you next door.'

'Is Pierre all right? Is he injured?'

'Only his pride. And I daresay that will recover pretty fast. In no time he will have seen off the raiders single-handed without losing the crease in his trousers.'

No love lost there, then. I let her boss me about and then she left my side to deal with the injured passengers. Bruce Everton also departed, mountain of reports to do, he said diplomatically. Helen gave me a short Conway blue cotton nightie to wear and put me to bed in Judith's own cabin next door. It had twin beds.

'So sorry,' she said. 'Change of plan. We need the private room in the medical centre for a lady who has broken her wrist rather badly. You'll be comfortable here.'

'Don't worry. I quite understand. I'll be fine.'

Suddenly, I was very tired. The day felt much longer than usual. Perhaps it had something to do with global warming and the earth's orbit slowing down. A couple of extra hours had been tagged on. Don't ask me where.

Judith's cabin was a lot like mine, except that everything was the other way round. I fell asleep wondering where the bathroom was. I would be needing it very soon. I had drunk a lot of water.

I was missing Sam. He had always been so supportive, as well as such a dish. The busy medical centre had made me think of him and I would not have been surprised if he had walked in through the door. However, he walked into my dreams instead and I had to make do with that.

Aggressive voices broke in on my dream and it spiralled away in fragments. There was arguing outside the door. I recognized the defensive, carping voice immediately.

'How was I to know what was going on? The noise was spoiling my speech of thanks and the audience was getting restless. And I was in the middle of fixing up a date with one of the singers in the girl group, the red-headed one.'

'You were fixing up a date with one of the girls in the middle of a raid on our ship?' It was Judith. She'd probably forgotten that I had been put to bed in her cabin. 'Sometimes you are beyond belief, Pierre. Typical. You think of nothing but yourself. But then, you always have.'

She knew him. It sounded as if she knew him from some time back. I could tell from her words, from the tone of her voice. 'I don't know what my sister saw in you,' she went on. 'Dazzled by that Gallic charm, I suppose. Well, she's well rid of you, and she knows it. You might have left her poorer than a church mouse but at least she's happy.'

'You were jealous,' said Pierre, swiftly turning the tables. 'You always were cheesed off because I preferred your younger sister, slim and gorgeous, to a dumpy sour-mouthed doctor. We used to laugh at you, the two of us, when we were in bed together, only a wall away from you. I expect you could hear us laughing.'

'I could hear you snoring.'

'Jealousy does funny things to people, especially ageing women.'

'I don't believe it,' said Judith, with a short laugh. 'You're making it up. I can always tell when you are lying. A red light comes on in the middle of your forehead.'

It was not a pretty conversation. Both voices were unpleasant. They obviously disliked each other intensely.

I hoped they couldn't hear me breathing. My breath sounded loud and rasping. I was all agog for more revelations about Pierre and Judith and the unknown sister. This might be a link to the deaths of Tracy Coleman and Lorna Fletcher. They had both died in the same way, garrotted by the same hand. Tracy had been deputy to Pierre. Lorna had a fear of open spaces, agoraphobia, and might have consulted Judith about her condition. Perhaps she needed some kind of medication to get as far as the dining room. It was like a dance, a minuet, with Pierre and Judith changing partners, coming close to sudden death, then parting again. Everything fuelled by their hatred of each other.

I would have made a note of this conversation, but I was practically armless, one arm professionally strapped up and the other sporting the saline drip. But I might be able to hold a pencil between my fingers at some uncomfortable angle.

It was complicated taking the whole saline drip apparatus along with me in the cabin, as I staggered over to Judith's desk. She'd be bound to have a pen or pencil. I had both in mine. The drawer didn't open easily. There seemed to be a roll of paper which had got caught in the runner.

I carefully eased it open. The voices had died away. Judith had gone back to her patients and Pierre had returned to his cabin to change and shower, and then I guessed he'd make straight for the nearest bar with his own story of the heroic hostage situation. He'd soon forget who got shot saving him. He'd lose no time in cashing in on the popularity stakes. The passengers would be generous in picking up the tab.

The rolls of paper uncurled on being released. I wasn't going to read them, but there they were in my hands. They were copies of medical reports on Tracy Coleman and Lorna Fletcher. What were they doing here, in Judith's desk drawer? Surely Lorna's should be amongst the medical records in the medical centre?

And Tracy had been employed by Conway. Her records should be at Head Office.

Judith's cabin did not seem such a safe haven after all. Nor was my own. Where could I go, wearing a blue cotton nightie?

The choice was overwhelming. There was DCI Bruce Everton, chief engineer Daniel Webster and security officer Edmund Morgan, in order of preference. They would all give up a bed to me, I felt sure. I also felt sure that Judith would lend me her bathrobe in the circumstances. There was probably a good reason why she had the records, but I didn't feel safe. I let myself out into the corridor, robe over my shoulders.

The corridors were bustling with passengers, coming and going, wearing odd assortments of clothes, so the bathrobe fitted in without any eyebrow lifting. Everyone was taking wet clothes to the laundry room or dry cleaners, both of which did a twenty-four-hour service. No one took any notice of me, all too busy swapping stories of their experiences.

'One of the officers is making a list in the Cairo Lounge.' Gina was broadcasting the good news. 'I've told him everything I've lost. You should go and see him. And he's got a box of jewellery that they have recovered.'

'Yes, I will. I will. Thank you for telling me. They took my opal engagement ring. It was my mother's. And my wedding ring and watch.'

'How awful,' Gina went on, talking as she walked. 'Mine were diamonds. And a lot of them. Worth a pretty fortune. I'll never see them again.'

But she had been shouting something quite different — that they were fakes — to the pirates. This was fishy. She was going to disclaim any recovered artificial diamonds when they were shown to her. She'd say her jewellery was real and was not amongst the recovered goods. She'd say it had gone overboard or was with the raiders. No doubt, they were fully insured.

Edmund's cabin was in the officer's quarters near the bridge. I'd not been there before, but it was part of his duties to give me sanctuary, wasn't it? A cabin steward was hovering with a trolley full of towels. He was running late, no doubt delayed by the fracas on deck.

'Can you let me into Edmund Morgan's cabin, please?' I asked, all sweetness and light. 'He said I could wait here, as the medical centre is full of casualties,' I said, the story running smoothly off my lips. It did not seem too much of a lie. Edmund would have said it, that is, if he knew about it.

'Of course, Miss Jones.' The steward was all smiles. 'You are brave lady, rescuing Monsieur Arbour from the raiders. And to be shot. You must rest. I shall bring you refreshments.'

'That's most kind,' I said as he unlocked the cabin door. 'But I am not hungry.'

'You must eat. Build up strength.'

Edmund's cabin was small but compact, with lots of dark polished wood, and tidy as a new pin. Apart from a few books and an alarm clock, it did not look occupied. The desk looked unused and housed only the notebook that he had filled on our information-gathering tour. I was not into peeking into the wardrobe or chest of drawers, but I did look into the bathroom. A disposable razor, a toothbrush and a bottle of Aramis aftershave. Expensive taste.

He'd said he was going to cross-reference every comment made in his notes. He did not appear to have made a start on it. The notes were a jumble.

I laid down on top of the bed, bone-weary. Even that short walk had worn me out. Yes, perhaps my strength did need building up. Two weeks' recuperation in my flat in sunny Worthing was the answer, watching the long tide wash in and out, walking the pier and chatting to the anglers, going to a few concerts, a few films. It sounded idyllic and it was, even when it rained.

There was a knock on the door. I hesitated. 'Who is it?'

'Hasid, Miss Jones. With some refreshments.'

It was too good to be true. I could not resist opening the door and it was, thankfully, the steward wheeling a trolley.

He smiled broadly.

'Some small foods for you. From the Boulevard Café late buffet.'

'How very kind. Thank you, Hasid. I really appreciate it.'

He brought in the trolley and parked it by the desk. 'You eat now and sleep well. Goodnight, Miss Jones. I will shut door.'

He left as silently as he had appeared. The trolley was laden with delightful savoury canapés, soup in a thermos, coffee in a jug, cold milk, yogurt and a bowl of fruit. There was even a dish of little sweets, petit fours, including candied ginger which is good for seasickness.

'Thank you, Hasid,' I breathed.

It was all lovely. I had some soup and some canapés before I dozed off into fragmented sleep. All in aid of building myself up. I was making an effort.

I heard the door open. It was probably Hasid with refills.

'Come in,' I said sleepily. 'That was really delicious. Thank you.'

'What are you doing in my cabin?' a voice snapped.

Edmund Morgan looked surprised and

angry, a sort of nervous tic appearing round the corner of his mouth. He filled the doorway, undecided whether to come in or go out.

'Hello, Edmund. I needed somewhere to sleep. I thought you wouldn't mind if I used your cabin, temporarily, of course.'

He didn't seem to notice that the blue nightgown was pretty short and there was a lot of tanned leg showing. He was not reacting like any normal man. Bruce and Daniel would have been kneeling at my bedside in five seconds flat.

Edmund was holding something behind his back. It was difficult to see what he was trying to hide. Then I caught a glint of metal and knew instantly. I recognized the weapon.

It was a gun. A sawn-off shotgun. The one which had fired at me. It had to be.

20

At Sea

It's not often that I panic, but I panicked at the sight of that gun.

'Don't shoot!' I cried. 'I'm already shot.'

'Don't be stupid, Casey,' he said. 'I'm not going to shoot you. I found the gun on deck. Someone else tried to shoot you. And it wasn't any of the raiders. They had automatics.'

'You mean it might have been one of the passengers? Surely not.'

'You were certainly not shot by one of the raiders. The line of fire was quite different. I don't know much about firearms, but I do know that the shot came from a different direction.'

'But you are holding the gun now. So how about fingerprints or DNA?'

'There might be something,' said Edmund putting it down gingerly on his desk. 'It ought to be in a plastic bag,' he agreed. 'Contamination, you know.'

Quite useless. He'd be security on a ferry boat next year.

'Well, it's very reassuring to know that I was shot by one of our own passengers and not by a raider,' I said. But the comment didn't register. How I longed to be back in my own cabin. I would pull the duvet over my head and not re-emerge until it was time for me to fly home. Surely they must have found a suitable replacement by now?

'So, how are the passengers?' I asked.

'Drowning their sorrows, having hysterics or fast emailing personal losses to their insurance company.'

'Nothing has changed, then?'

'Except that we have a captured gang of raiders on board, and I don't know what to do with them. Some of them got away.'

'Put them ashore at the next port of call. Let the local police deal with them.'

'As always,' said Edmund, 'you are full of common sense.'

'I'm also very tired and would like to go to sleep.'

'Yes, of course,' he said, backing off. 'You go to sleep. I'll be back later.'

★   ★   ★

I have no idea if he did come back later because, after a nap, I dismantled the drip and took off for my own cabin. I was quite capable of drinking a glass of water without the aid of a tube.

The cabin, even my temporary one, seemed like home. I locked the door against all intruders, propped a chair against the handle, made some coffee and then got out a sheet of paper and a pen. I had to write down everything that had happened to see if I could spot some sort of sense or order.

1. Tracy Coleman disappeared.
2. Tracy found dead, head injury, garrotted.
3. Lorna Fletcher cheated at quiz.
4. Lorna found dead, garrotted, made to look like suicide.

5. Pirates raid ship.
6. I get shot.
7. Suspects:

I paused. I had no real suspects. Even if the victim had been taken by surprise, she would have struggled. And it must be someone who had access to Conway neck scarves or took Tracy's. They needed frequent laundering, so I had a stock.

Romanoff had been having an affair with Tracy but seemed genuinely distressed by her death. He had cancelled several of his concerts and when he appeared on deck, his face was haggard and gaunt.

Gina had bought Pierre expensive jewellery, but did that mean anything, apart from some seedy explanation? Equally, Lorna Fletcher had a secret life, but it was not enough to be a motive. Her husband had a strong alibi for when his wife died. He was in a bar with the MacDonalds and Ted Sullivan and was seen by several passengers.

None of it made any sense. And I didn't think Bruce Everton had been any more successful with his investigations. He would surely have confided in me if he had discovered anything of importance. Or would he? He had been too preoccupied to spend much time with me recently.

There was an urgent knock. I heard his voice outside my door.

'Let me in, Casey. Unlock Fort Knox, please. I know you are in there. I think I've got a breakthrough.'

This was too good to miss. I pulled the bathrobe round me and got off my bed. I unlocked the door and moved the chair. For a second, I hesitated. Suppose it was someone who only sounded like Bruce?

'Bruce?' I asked uncertainly.

'You have every right to be extra careful, Casey,' he said. 'But it is me, and I can prove it. Would it be the act of a cad to remind you of a goodnight kiss that knocked me out for six?'

I opened the door with my good hand. 'Me, too,' I said. 'Knocked out.'

Bruce was standing in the corridor, smiling. 'Good.'

He came in. He had the unwashed,

unslept look of half the crew and quite a few of the passengers. We were going to have to work hard to get back to the scrupulously high standard of the Conway Blue Line.

'How are you?' He took in my arm in a collar and the wrist sling. 'No drip?'

'Not wanted on voyage.'

'Take it easy, Casey. Don't rush back into work. You have been injured.'

I found half a smile from somewhere. 'This is taking it easy.'

Bruce came into my cabin, his keen eyes raking in the list and the coffee and the state of undress. I wrapped the bathrobe more firmly round me. I didn't want anyone getting ideas.

'While you were in the medical centre, I went on to the NID. They let me use the computer terminals in the purser's office these days. Very helpful. It takes a bit of time, but it came up with some useful information.'

'The NID? What's that stand for?'

'Everything is reduced to an acronym these days. It stands for National Injuries Database. It's managed by the National

Police Improvement Agency at Wyboston, Bedfordshire, bless their rural cotton socks. It has more than twenty thousand images from four thousand cases, mostly suspicious ones.'

'It sounds amazing.'

'There's no other database like it in the world. You can search for injuries that match the case you are working on. You know how profilers pick on similarities? I thought these two deaths were very strange. Garrotting with a silk scarf, hiding other injuries.'

'You mean, they have found others that match these injuries?'

'You're pretty quick, Miss Jones. They have found two other cases, one an assault and the other a fatality, but both were garrotting with a silk scarf to cover a different injury.'

'Four cases,' I breathed. 'The assault case, does that mean the victim survived?'

'Yes, she survived that attack. She was a member of a ship's entertainment crew. Her name was Tracy Coleman, and it was when she was working on another cruise ship line, one of the giant ones. They've a dozen ships. Won't mention the household name. She was assaulted but managed to survive.'

'Was it our Tracy Coleman?'

'The same.

'But not so lucky this time.' Poor Tracy Coleman. 'And the fatality?'

'Another cruise death. This was a first-class passenger called Sally Newman. A widow. Same big line. And at about the same time. Still checking date of cruise.'

This presented an entirely different picture. Now we had four similar crimes with cruise ships as their location. I could see the work ahead.

'So now we have to check crew and passenger lists of those cruises and this cruise. We have to see if the same name comes up on both?'

'But people can change their name. Get a new passport by devious means. Of course, they can't change their appearance without extensive surgery.'

Bruce sat down heavily on my only armchair. I was still perched on the bed. He looked worn out. I got up and made him some coffee with my good arm, but when I came back, he was fast asleep, looking most uncomfortable.

Somehow, with one arm, I heaved him to his feet and steered him, sleepwalking, towards my bed. He fell on it, sprawled all over the place, never waking. He was out for the count. I took off his shoes and socks, loosened his belt and top trouser button, loosened his shirt-collar buttons and then pushed him over to the far side of the bed, against the wall. No further intimacy. He was still asleep.

It was hardly the most romantic of moments, but I slid onto the bed beside him and wrapped myself in his arms. I could dream, couldn't I?

★   ★   ★

He had gone when I awoke. No little note. It might never have happened. Nothing did happen. It had been the sleep of innocents. But the duvet had been pulled up over my shoulders.

I was unsure of my status now. Pierre had dismissed me from all duties, except boring office-confined typing. But I was officially walking wounded, status: heroine. And I couldn't type efficiently with one hand. And there were these lists of crew and passengers to check. It had to be done straight away.

★   ★   ★

I had a leisurely shower with a plastic bag wrapped round the dressing on my arm. I looked out the cabin window, wrapped in a bath towel, making my first cup of tea. There was a light mist and rain spattering the glass. The weather had changed. We were on our way to St Lucia, where it rained a lot.

All I could remember of St Lucia from previous visits was that it grew sixty-five different types of mangoes and its last earthquake was in 1980. And I knew, from the locals, that a long line of wave is dangerous.

I put on my uniform. The hardest part was doing up a bra with one hand. In the end I had to step into it and pull it up. I began to appreciate having the use of both hands. My makeup was weird. I gave up and left Nature to do its best.

There were lots of comments from passengers on my way to the office. They were all kind comments and I had to stop and reassure them that I was recovering.

'But you are not working, surely?' They were astonished.

The office was empty. Debbie and Gary were already out on deck, refereeing various games. The port lecturer was in full swing with colour slides of the Piton Peaks. Other lecturers were carrying on, keeping to their programmes. Pierre was nowhere to be seen. Obviously still recovering from his hostage ordeal.

I had a computer terminal to myself. I emailed Head Office, reassuring them that I was alive and well, but I asked them if it was possible to get the crew and passenger lists of the cruises which Bruce had mentioned.

'I know this is unethical,' I emailed, 'but the information is urgently required by DCI Bruce Everton, who is in charge of the investigations here. Surely you must have some access? We really need it.'

They asked me to wait, agog with curiosity.

While I waited, I looked into Tracy Coleman's files. Yes, she had worked for the other line. There was nothing suspicious about that, except that she had requested a double lock on her cabin door. It hadn't done her much good.

Head Office was so efficient. They emailed back reams of names, but said that it had cost them a mile high of favours and that I would be top of the list fulfilling those favours. I didn't understand this part, but gathered that I would pay for it later.

I had one black coffee after another as I checked these lists against the lists we had for the *Aveline*. Names began to blur. All the Smiths and Jones and Robinsons. Then one name stood out. It shone in neon.

I had to talk to Bruce. I phoned him, tannoyed, emailed, began to panic when I couldn't get hold of him. Then he answered.

'Yes, Casey. What is it?'

'We have a serial killer on board.'

21

At Sea

There was no way we could confront the man. Bruce agreed that we had to lay low until he showed his hand again. Though this was the last thing we ever wanted to happen.

It was in a sober mood that we went up on deck. The Caribbean was curiously quiet and iridescent, its blueness so vivid that it almost hurt the eyes.

'It's difficult to believe that we are sailing through such beauty with such a monster on board,' I said.

'It's the same all the world over,' said Bruce. 'It's God's country and yet terrible deeds are happening all the time. I see enough of it and that's only London. I have to leave you now. I must inform Captain Wellington immediately, to keep him up to date.'

'Will he be able to do anything?'

Bruce shook his head. 'We have no proof. It's all circumstantial. All we can do is tell him that we have discovered a link and hope that the authorities back in England have some forensic or DNA evidence from the Sally Newman case that could lead to an arrest.'

The only way to keep my mind straight was to knuckle down to some work and keep out of his way. To give him a wide berth. It would be difficult to act naturally, as if I knew nothing. As Bruce had said, we had no proof. It was only circumstantial that the man in question had been on board all the cruises where women had been garrotted. If he was questioned, he might have solid alibis for all the murders.

I hoped he had. The man was likeable in a strange way. The thought loitered in my mind that we might be wrong. It could be someone else.

'Hello, Casey.' It was Gina. She was looking sleek in a long chiffon dress with matching coat in two shades of lilac, trimmed with silk. Her sandals toned. She had even painted her toenails the same shade. She had been to the beauty salon despite the pirates' disruptions the previous evening. No depression here.

'Gina. You're looking very smart.'

'No point in letting life get you down. How's your arm?'

'Sore.'

'I'm not surprised. You were lucky it didn't hit the bone.'

'How do you know that?'

She wore a smile tacked on with nails. 'Lucky guess. Must go, dear. Meeting a friend for coffee. Can't be late.'

Gina was gone in a lilac swirl to her assignation, leaving a trail of perfume that nearly choked me. There was nothing subtle about her choice of scent. She probably bought it in pint bottles, mail order.

In the distance, on the surface of the sea, I saw an arc of silver, then another. It was a dolphin leaping into the air, with all the joy of a free creature, enjoying the sunlight and the sea. Dolphins often followed ships for the company. It was unspeakably moving and lifted my feelings. I smiled without thinking.

Some of the passengers had spotted the dolphins and there was a surge to the starboard side to take photos and videos. It was always an exhilarating sight and it never failed to delight me. The cruise line ought to put the dolphins on the payroll.

I checked with the office that all the morning's activities were in hand and made a circuitous route to the purser's department. I had my letter of permission from the captain. It didn't say anything about using computer terminals, but I hoped that they wouldn't want to read what it said too closely.

Fortunately they were overloaded with work following last night's chaos and simply waved me to a free terminal. A young female officer even brought me a cup of coffee. 'You look as if you need it,' she said, nodding towards my sling.

I began hacking into a bank account, using the information which Bruce had passed to me. Hacking is only illegal if the intent is fraudulent. Bruce had told me that a case taken to the House of Lords was overturned on the grounds that simple hacking did not constitute forgery.

This was simple hacking. I only wanted information. The crooks know how to do it, especially if their victims bank online.

I didn't ask Bruce how he got the security numbers. Scotland Yard had its mysterious ways.

The numbers. This individual had over half a million pounds in various banks. I looked at the incoming payments. There were regular amounts of £500, £300 and £100. Several were for £1,000. They were nothing like a salary or wages which usually have so much deducted for national insurance and pension funds. They were perfectly round sums, and some were cash payments. They looked fishy. Not dolphin fishy, dead-cod fishy.

I clicked print and, thank you, nice printer machine, copies of the pages I had marked came out in seconds onto the tray. And there were other bank accounts in his name with the same pattern. Round sums paid in at regular intervals. Bruce was going to be interested.

The *Aveline* was programmed for an overnight stay at St Lucia. We had a reciprocal arrangement with a big hotel on the coast. Passengers could book to have a night ashore at the hotel, and we hosted a party of visitors from the hotel who could enjoy a tour round the ship and dinner in the Zanzibar Dining Room. Minibuses were laid on for all the journeys involved.

It was always a popular arrangement. Pierre would not demean himself to act as a guide, whereas I liked showing off the wonders of a luxury cruise ship, answering questions, knowing that I was talking to possible future customers. I had my little patter about the history of ship design. 'Ships have always been designed to look like the houses and buildings that people leave behind. They are a series of floating rooms so that passengers feel secure when travelling. The decor is similar or better than our passengers have at home.

'So we have areas that look like English conservatories, bars that look like Bavarian hunting lodges, dining rooms like French palaces and indoor pools like Roman baths.' This usually raised a laugh.

'And it's not just cruise ships,' I'd go

on. 'The *Implacable*, a seventy-four-gun ship built in 1800, had stern carvings over four decks high that made it look like a tall building. This carving was saved and is now on the wall inside the entrance to the Maritime Museum at Greenwich.'

'What happened to the ship?' someone was bound to ask.

'The *Implacable* was scuttled in the English Channel on 2 December 1949,' I'd conclude, bringing the sorry tale to an end.

'Why?'

'Lack of money after the war. I think they had bands playing and flags flying to make it a worthy occasion.'

Yes, I would definitely get the tour. I was a natural. I might even volunteer for the brownie points.

I wasn't sure where the day went. My arm was starting to hurt; I wasn't resting it properly. Bruce and I pored over the bank statements in a secluded corner of the Boulevard Café. Crested peaks of waves followed the white wake in a soothing rhythm.

'There's a pattern,' he said. 'Look at

the dates. The smaller sums are erratic, but the five hundred pounds is regular on the last day of each month.'

'Could it be the interest from some investment or a regular sum withdrawn?'

'It would never be a round sum. There are always deductions for management fees or a change of interest rates. No, he's getting the five hundred pounds from the same source every month, either from one person or a company group.'

'What for?'

'It looks like a sophisticated blackmail racket. I'd guess he's collecting a handout every month to keep quiet about something. The smaller sums are one-off payments, sometimes in cash. But he is a man who doesn't throw his money about with high living. He prefers to bank it and watch his money grow.'

'Not these days.'

'It must be hurting. But look at these payments out to a betting shop. The man likes the horses.'

'And how do you think this all ties in with the deaths?'

'Maybe Tracy Coleman found out

about his extra financial activities and threatened to expose him. He couldn't have that happen, so there was enough motivation to silence her.'

'It's possible. And this Sally Newman, the widow? We know nothing about her, whether she was a passenger also being blackmailed or if she had to be silenced because she found out about him.' I couldn't see how we were going to find out. 'What about Lorna Fletcher, poor lady?'

'I think he approached her for a handout. We know she had been cheating in a very minor way in the quiz game, but he thought he could get something out of her to keep her quiet on the cruise. You know, being sent to Coventry on a cruise would not be pleasant. But he hadn't reckoned on her spirit and maybe she threatened to go to the captain.'

'She had phobias, a fear of people and a fear of open spaces. Agoraphobia. It would take a lot of courage.'

Bruce was looking at me with a strange expression. 'Casey, I know you are in peak mental condition, despite your arm.

And you have a lot of courage.'

'I don't like the sound of that,' I said. I suddenly craved the safety of my own sofa in Worthing. I had a long pale apple-green sofa that I could sit on sideways and stretch my legs out, easing the pain in my ankle. It was like a friend, always welcoming.

'The only way we are going to catch him is to set a trap. We need bait. Attractive female bait. We need someone to do something wrong, criminal, dubious, something dishonest or immoral. Then we'll wait until Mr Nasty approaches with a financial arrangement to ensure his utter silence and diplomacy.'

'Don't look at me like that.' I attempted to choke silently.

'Casey, please. I won't let anything happen to you.'

'I don't want to do this. Haven't I been through enough? Look, someone shot at me, tried to injure me or kill me. My job is arranging the entertainment. Bait doesn't get a bonus.'

'Tracy won't get a bonus, either. You

said yourself that he was a serial killer. How many more, Casey? We have got to catch him.' Bruce leaned forward and took my hand. It was warm and firm against my cold skin. 'You could do it. Any way you like. I won't leave you for a moment.'

That was quite tempting to have Bruce constantly at my side. If Sam wasn't around, he would have to be second best. Nothing had to happen.

'Dishonest or immoral?' he asked.

'Immoral, of course,' I said, leaning on a sigh. 'Far more fun.'

22

St Lucia

I only said immoral to lighten the atmosphere, but Bruce took it seriously. It sounded like one of those old-fashioned divorce cases where a prostitute provided the evidence and they sat on either side of the bed playing cards. Didn't Henry VIII play cards all night with the imported queen number four that he didn't fancy?

I thought I would have a choice of a partner in crime. But Bruce said no to Captain Wellington and definitely no to Chief Engineer Daniel Webster. They were my first and second choices, high on the list. The disappointment showed on my face momentarily.

'Not blackmail material,' he said. 'More like perfectly natural assignations. I'll fix it up for you. Something special, some-thing positively immoral.'

I thought I had been spectacularly dim

and was going to need a three-week coma to survive this. 'Not Judith Skinner? I'd say no to Judith or her chief nurse. You are not going to drag them into this.'

'Hardly raise an eyebrow these days,' said Bruce.

We were up early, passing the end of the airport runway of St Lucia on our port side. We saw the twin peaks in the distant mist. 'Stand by below' was rung to the engine control room as we approached the buoyed entrance channel. The first mooring lines were sent to the berth soon after, and all lines berthing the *Aveline* were soon fast.

The wide harbour of Port Castries was bustling with other cruise ships, white flags flying, merchant ships and ferries. Passengers were up early, anxious to go ashore. There were lots of shops, boutiques, markets and an Internet café close at hand. Not to mention numerous bars and cafés. There were also lots of traffic jams, as the rush hour tried to negotiate the narrow side streets.

'I'd like to go ashore,' I said.

'You're staying here,' Bruce said firmly.

'Don't worry. Go back to your cabin and undress. Put on something loose and comfortable.'

'I haven't got anything loose and comfortable.'

'Put on your bathrobe. You are going to be compromised.'

'There's no way out but death,' I said. It was a quote from somewhere, but I was not sure where. Sounded like Shakespeare.

*   *   *

I was not sure how this trap was going to work. I was to be caught in a compromising situation, then blackmailed. Clearly, I would not resist the blackmail — no garrotting, thank you — but promise to pay, make out a cheque, etc, or have loads of cash ready. Tearfully, of course. This would be filmed, videoed, CCTVed or whatever Bruce rigged up to get the evidence. I'd be accepted for RADA at this rate. A new career loomed.

How this would lead to the man's arrest over the murders was up to the authorities and their forensic evidence. Perhaps they hoped he might confess. This kind of situation never occurred in my initial training sessions. I ought to send Head Office a memo.

I had a quick shower in case I didn't get another chance. It was strange how nervous I felt, far more nervous than walking onto a stage in front of a crowd of people. I hoped Bruce had not chosen some airhead celebrity for this escapade. We had a few on board. Maybe we would watch some in-house television, have a cup of coffee, make small talk.

There was a knock on my cabin door and I took a deep breath. The moment had come. I had to go through with it. There was Tracy to think of, and Lorna Fletcher and the unknown Sally Newman. I was doing it for them.

Hasid stood in the corridor with a laden trolley. He smiled at me. It was an innocent smile on his handsome face.

'Refreshments, Miss?'

'Yes, thank you. Please bring the trolley in.' It was serious head-nodding time. Was he part of the plan, or was I simply being offered more food? Did I need building up again?

He paused in the doorway. Had Bruce told him anything? Did he know that he was risking his job? An assignation with a steward, especially a steward from overseas, was a serious offence. I could lose my job, and so could he.

He wheeled the trolley in and stood, waiting. He was waiting to be asked if he should pour the coffee. I nodded, at the same time dialling Bruce's mobile phone number. 'Yes, please, Hasid. Please pour the coffee. Would you like some?'

'Thank you, Miss.'

'Hello?' Bruce answered.

'Is this right? A delivery of refreshments that I didn't order? You know this could be a serious offence? It's not on. He could lose his job.'

'Don't worry about him. He won't get into trouble. Offer the young steward a coffee, but don't drink any yourself.'

'Is that all?' I was indignant.

'That's all you need to know.'

I was shocked. No way would I get this

young man into trouble. It was unacceptable. Bring on the airhead celebrity. I would tell Hasid to go back to his duties. I put down the phone and turned.

But it was too late. This young man was enjoying the novelty of a coffee in the company of a female member of the entertainment department. And a female member in her bathrobe and with wet hair. He knew that he shouldn't, but it would be something to talk about in the canteen with his friends. The crew lived on cabin gossip.

'No, don't . . . ' I said. But it was too late. Hasid put down the cup unsteadily. He was already looking strange; his eyes wavering round the cabin. I knew immediately what had been done. The coffee had been drugged. Something quick-acting.

I caught Hasid as he staggered and fell. He was slightly built and I could take his weight, even with only one good arm. It was not difficult to drag him over to the bed and let him fall onto it. He was out for the count. But he was breathing normally and did not seem distressed. I hoped it was something he could sleep off. Something that would not harm him.

I poured myself some pineapple juice from the trolley. I'd have words with Bruce about this. It was not fair to Hasid. I hoped Hasid was going to get a big bonus. I could ring Bruce again . . . if I knew where the phone . . . and Bruce's number . . . what . . . was . . . his . . . number . . .

★   ★   ★

I awoke some time later. I was also on the bed. It was a single bed with hardly room for two grown people, so Hasid was close. Too close. He was snoring lightly.

I looked at his face. He was a dead ringer for a baby angel. I would make sure that he did not get into trouble. I emptied out two water bottles in the bathroom and filled one with the cold coffee from his cup and the other with the pineapple juice from my glass. I dated both of them. This evidence might be needed.

He was still asleep when I left the cabin

and went on deck. I had no idea of the time. It was an overnight stay in St Lucia, but which day was it now? How long had I slept? Who had put me on the bed with the young steward?

I was seething. The first person to speak to me was going to get an earful, and Bruce would get more than an earful. It was Daniel Webster, taking a break from his engines, and he knew nothing about any of this.

'Casey? You're looking better. How are you feeling?'

'Still sore. Had a good night's sleep,' I added ironically. 'When do we depart?'

'At six p.m., but all on board by five thirty p.m. Are you going ashore, Casey? No? Would you like to come with me for a drink and a stroll round the harbour? Nothing too strenuous.'

A drink and a stroll with this pleasant young officer would be normal and nautical miles away from the lunacy that I was involved in now. I found one of my grade-A smiles for him. 'That sounds good,' I said. It was the third time he'd asked me out. 'Let me know when you are free.'

'I'll phone you.'

'I'll put on strolling clothes.'

'You'd look great in anything.'

My morale shot sky high. I rose from the ashes. I was myself again. My confidence returned and I knew I would survive whatever happened in the next few hours. I sat on deck, near the Boulevard Café, nursing an un-doctored coffee and a croissant with a pat of butter. To hell with calories.

Edmund came and sat beside me. He had a laden tray with his usual fry-up. 'OK if I join you?'

'Sure. Is that your breakfast or a late supper? Or both?'

'I've been up working half the night. All these compensation claims after the raid. I have to initial them as correct, and of course, I have no way of knowing if the claims are right.'

'Oh dear. It must be difficult.'

'I've even got a box of jewellery left over, all unclaimed. How can passengers not know what they were wearing? I've got watches, earrings, necklaces.'

I didn't really know. 'I suppose if you wear the same rings, day in and day out, or the same watch or gold chain necklace, you forget exactly what. You could have an auction at the end of the cruise and give the money to the sailors' benevolent fund.'

'That's it, good idea,' said Edmund, shovelling eggs and bacon in to his mouth, followed by hash browns. 'No one really knows what they've got.'

I let him get on with his breakfast. The sun was rising and the first warm rays were flooding the decks. Even the deck runners had finished and were staggering towards the café for water and juice.

'Do you ever run, Edmund?'

'Once upon a time. But not now. Sadly, it's called encroaching old age. Old Father Time and all that.'

He leaned towards me and pushed a handful of photographs in my direction. I didn't need to know what they were. But how did he get them? They were shots of me, in a gaping bathrobe, close to Hasid, bare arms and legs entwined.

'So what's this?' I said. The words came from nowhere.

'So, Casey,' he said, spearing a hash-brown. 'Not quite the cold ice maiden that you pretend to be. Like young boys, do you, with a brown skin? This looks like quite a hot session and with a young cabin steward. Tut, tut, Casey. This could ruin your career. It will certainly ruin your career if it gets out to Head Office. And, of course, the boy will never work with Conway Blue Line again, or any other cruise line. Back to the fields for him.'

Edmund Morgan, security officer. So inept. So inefficient. So useless. But there was one thing that he was adept at, it seemed: Blackmail.

'Where did you get these?'

'They were put under my door. You have an enemy, my dear. No prizes for guessing who.'

'Are you going to give them to me?' I said, my hand on the photographs.

'Good heavens, no. They are worth quite a bit. Five hundred, in cash.'

'For heaven's sake, you're joking. I don't have it.'

'I suggest you find it, and pretty quick. You earn a good salary.'

His eyes were no longer mild; they were now glinting with undisguised greed.

'I'll go ashore and get the money,' I said, my words all mumbled. I didn't know what I was saying. Where was Bruce? I needed rescuing. Croissant crumbs fell onto my lap.

'That's my girl,' he said mildly.

'I'm not your girl.' Ripples of sick panic shot through me.

'Oh, yes, you are. You belong to me now. And I've made copies of the photographs. Destroying these won't be the end, either. You're mine till the end of your natural days. You're going to be paying for your little roll in the hay forever and ever.'

23

St Lucia

'I told you that I wouldn't leave your side,' said Bruce. There was a split second of softness. 'And I didn't, not from the moment that you passed out. I heaved you up and put you on the bed so at least you were comfortable. I was with you all the time, till you began to wake up.'

'Heaved me up? What kind of language is that?'

'Sorry. You're quite tall.'

'You took those photographs,' I choked.

'Yes. Sorry about that, but here are the negatives. You can have them. You can destroy them.'

'I'll never forgive you.'

'I'm sorry if that's how you feel, but you did agree to help catch this killer. I didn't say it would be easy.'

It was true. I should have known that it wouldn't be a piece of cake. 'What about

Hasid? I don't want him to get into trouble.'

'It's all been covered. As far as anyone knows, he was taken sick and spent the night in the crew sick bay. He'll remember nothing about passing out in your cabin. Hopefully all he will remember is delivering the trolley to your cabin and then waking up in the sick bay.'

'Is that a promise?'

'A promise.'

'And what about my meeting with Edmund this morning? Was it filmed?'

'No, but there was a bug under the table. We have recorded the conversation. It's all on tape.'

'How did you know which table I would sit at?' I was beginning to relax, hoping for a non-scary answer. 'I could have sat anywhere.'

Bruce could not help grinning. 'We bugged all the tables. You'd be surprised at morning table talk. Good thing I'm not into extortion. I could make a fortune and retire on the proceeds.'

'And when will you arrest Edmund?' I wanted the man under lock and key. I didn't want to feel a scarf tightening round my neck.

'When you hand the money over to him. He has to be caught in the act. If we arrest him now, he could say that it's a big lie and you made it all up.'

'Sure, like I made up the photos? I suppose you slipped them under his door?'

'Sorry. I couldn't think of any other way of getting them to him.'

'So he'll think they were from his accomplice?'

'Probably, if there is one. We don't know.'

'Supposing he checks?'

'Ah . . . let's hope that he doesn't. It could get complicated. Don't worry, Casey. Your part is nearly over. You only have to hand him the money. And I have the cash here for you.' He patted his pocket. 'I'll give it to you when you've made the arrangements to meet him again.'

'Do I have to meet him again?'

'Only once more.'

'I think I'll jump ship with the five

hundred, buy some nice clothes and head for home. Business class, of course.'

'I might come with you.'

I didn't know if he was joking. His private life was still a mystery. He seemed to like me a lot, but cruise ships have that romantic atmosphere for any age. Maybe he was sowing a few wild oats, if a little on the late side. Happiness is a choice and maybe he never had a choice. This was not the time to ask him.

'I'll book you a seat.'

'Are you going to the medical centre this morning? That dressing ought to be looked at. I'm sure Judith will fit you in without an appointment.'

He was right. I thought I could feel a throb in my arm and that was not good. I'd been trying to ignore it. I'd be in trouble if an infection had set in. Judith Skinner would be jabbing me with antibiotics.

'I'll keep in touch,' I said, getting up unsteadily.

Judith Skinner was not happy when she removed the dressing. 'It looks a bit nasty, though all the stitches are still in place,' she said, peering close. 'What have you been doing?'

'Nothing.'

'Did you get any sleep?'

I nodded. 'Sort of.'

'Perhaps you've knocked it. There's no muscle damage. Does this hurt?'

'Ouch.'

'I'll start you on a course of antibiotics to be on the safe side. Take them all, finish the course.' She wrote out a prescription. 'Take this out to Helen and she'll get the tablets for you from the dispensary.'

'Sorry about the drip.'

'Damned things,' said Judith.

Helen bustled with the prescription to the drugs cabinet. 'Let's see what we can find for you, Casey. Soon have you fit again. Everyone is talking about the pirate raid, you know. You're a real heroine.'

'I don't feel like a heroine.'

'It took some guts to face the raiders like that.'

'I don't remember much about it. Instinct, I guess.'

'You'll be getting rows of gold stars

from Head Office.' She found the prescribed antibiotics and labelled the packet with my name. 'Take one immediately, then one every six hours for five days. Please finish the course.'

'Thanks.'

Helen made a neat job of putting on a fresh dressing. I noticed her ring. It was a dull old gold ring with an opal in an ornate setting. I thought nurses didn't wear jewellery on duty because of germs.

'My mother's engagement ring,' she said hurriedly. 'I forgot to take it off.'

It was time for a late breakfast. I had not eaten anything since the crumbled croissant. And I had only sipped at a coffee while sitting with Edmund Morgan. I'd been too stressed to eat.

Dining staff were clearing away the breakfast buffet, but I managed to get the last of the scrambled eggs and mushrooms. One of the stewards carried my tray and another followed with a cup of coffee.

'Very brave lady,' he said with the faintest wink.

'Please stop saying that.'

'You certain to get medal,' said the other one.

I smiled back. I might as well enjoy the glory before I went back to work. Most of the passengers were enjoying their second day in St Lucia, so there was not much work to do. It was a lovely island and there were lots of beaches to visit. Debbie and Gary were getting on famously and I knew I would be sending in glowing reports for both of them. I could see Gary being promoted one day. He didn't plan on being a DJ forever and would make a good deputy.

Pierre was apparently still in a state of shock. A state of shock which needed copious refills of Pimm's to steady his nerves. He was in the Bridge Bar regaling everyone with his version of events. When I enquired how he was feeling, he didn't answer or even bother to thank me for saving him.

'You're not properly dressed,' he said, barely glancing at me. 'Put your full uniform on.'

'I can't do up the shirt buttons with one hand,' I said.

'Excuses, excuses. Do the buttons up before you put it on.'

'I can't pull it over my head with one arm in a sling.'

He had a black eye which was turning a lurid shade of orange and green. I did not comment on it. And I could see strands of grey on his forehead where he had not been able to touch up the roots to their customary black sheen.

'I'm sure you'll be glad to know that the entertainment department is running smoothly,' I said. 'And that things are back to normal. Will you be introducing tonight's show?'

I didn't wait to hear the answer. I could see the indecision lapping like waves across his face. He wanted to introduce the show, but he also wanted to continue milking the hostage situation. It was worth a few drinks more.

My phone was ringing. I moved away to a window to answer it. I guessed it would be Bruce with an appointment with the death-watch devil.

'Hello?'

'Casey?'

'Sorry, Casey is not here at the moment,' I said. 'She is with Captain Wellington, helping to steer the ship. Please ring back later.'

'Don't be silly, Casey. I know it's you. Edmund wants to see you in his office immediately.'

'How do you know?'

'He's emailed you.'

'You're reading my emails?' Clouds like bruises were gathering in the sky. It was going to rain. The tour of passengers visiting the rum distillers would be happy. Time for a few more tasters. Some of the mother tanks were 95 per cent alcohol.

'Not exactly. I'm reading his emails.'

'I'm not going into his office. That's final. Full stop. Finale.'

'Casey, it's only for a few moments to hand over the money. You'll be bugged. I'll be outside the door. He can't hurt you.'

'You think you can guarantee that?'

'Think of Tracy, Mrs Fletcher and the unknown Sally Newman.'

'I am thinking of them and what happened to them.'

There was a silence. I knew Bruce was disappointed in me, but I couldn't suddenly become Joan of Arc. I felt a tight edge of sadness. I was letting him down. For some reason I thought of mangrove trees growing through ramshackle shacks and steel drains. My mind was in a turmoil, half on this Caribbean island, the other half drowning in fear.

'OK, I'll go,' I said, my voice lost somewhere down in my trainers.

'That's great,' said Bruce. 'I'll meet you in the Boulevard Café, at the far corner table, starboard. Ten minutes.'

'Starboard? Star bright, star right?'

'Well done, Casey. You can still remember then?'

I had ten minutes to get myself into gear. Not clothes gear, mind gear. I wanted everything to be finished so I could go home. To hell with the annual assessment. They could keep cruising. I'd become a manager at some yacht club on the south coast. There were plenty of them.

Those ten minutes were spent wisely. I did change my clothes, put on my full-deck uniform, even the jacket, despite the heat. It meant throwing off the sling for a while, but I managed. Immaculate make-up followed. I dusted rouge with a big brush to disguise the pallor. But I wasn't wasting my favourite perfume on Edmund. I used a sample spray of old stock from the ship's shop.

Bruce was waiting. The customary coffee was waiting. I didn't even sit down.

'Just give me the money and the bug and I'll be off,' I said tersely.

'Casey, it's not as easy as that. I have to brief you. Tell you what to say. It's important if the tape is to be used as evidence.'

Bruce was back in police mode, no expression on his face. He pushed a slim envelope towards me and I put it in my jacket pocket. It didn't even make a bulge. Fifty-pound notes, I guessed. Ten of them.

'This is the bug,' he said. 'Put it inside your clothes and clip the microphone to your bra strap so that it's not visible. Clip the on and off switch to your waistband. Don't forget to switch it on.'

'I can do all that. You don't need to tell me.'

'Don't forget to mention the five hundred pounds out loud. Say it's for the incriminating photos. Remind him that he demanded that amount from you. We must have every step of the transaction. Don't simply hand it over, saying, 'Here it is'.'

'I was going to say, 'Up yours, guv'.'

'Hardly appropriate in the circumstances, Casey, however strongly you feel.'

'Can I go now?'

'You're still annoyed with me?'

'Yes. I didn't think it would be like this. I don't know what I thought it would be like, but not like this.'

The bug was bundled into my other jacket pocket and I marched off to the nearest ladies' cloakroom. The anger and indignation were inexplicable but the feelings were real. I wanted to get it over. There was no fear, despite the fact that I was dealing with a possible murderer. It hadn't been proved.

The tiny microphone clipped to my bra strap felt huge, scratching my skin, but it didn't show. I switched it on.

'You OK, Casey?' said Daniel Webster, passing me in a corridor as I went down in to the depths towards Edmund's office.

'Fine,' I said, brightly. 'Back on track.'

'Captain Wellington would like you to dine at his table this evening,' he went on. 'I'm supposed to deliver the invitation.'

'How kind,' I said. 'I'd be delighted. Formal?'

'As formal as you like.'

Would it be my pink Versace or my black fishtail chiffon? It depended which looked best with an arm dressing and a wrist and collar sling. Maybe the silver trouser suit was the best cover-up.

I knocked on the door of Edmund's office but didn't wait for an answer. I went straight in. He looked up from his desk, surprised, perhaps not expecting me so promptly.

'I've brought the five hundred pounds that you demanded from me for keeping quiet about the incriminating photographs taken in my cabin last night without my permission.' I said it all in one breath. 'You don't have to count the money. It's all there.'

'Sit down, Casey,' he said. 'We don't have to hurry this.'

'Yes, we do have to hurry this. I don't want to be breathing the same air as you for one moment longer than I have to. How many other people have you blackmailed like this? Did you blackmail Tracy and Mrs Fletcher and Sally Newman?'

His face tightened, a tic showing at the corner of his mouth. 'What's all this? Sally Newman? How do you know about Sally Newman?'

'Was she a friend of yours or simply another unfortunate passenger?'

'I don't think it is any of your business,' he said, standing up. His hands were splayed on top of the desk. 'Hand over the money and we'll call this matter finished.'

'Where are the photographs?'

'In my safe. And that's where they will stay until we dock at Southampton. I'll return them to you then.'

'But I'm not staying on the ship until Southampton. I'll be returning to the UK as soon as they have found a replacement for me.'

We were getting into muddy waters. And I had a grim feeling that I had said too much in the heat of the moment. Perhaps I shouldn't have mentioned the other three women.

'This one's going to be trouble,' said another voice from behind me, a woman's voice. 'I knew she was going to be as soon as she spotted the ring. I shouldn't have worn it. A big mistake. But we won't make any more mistakes, will we, Eddie?'

Suddenly there was a bare arm across my throat. No silken scarf, but bone and flesh pressing down on my larynx.

I gasped and started struggling, but the woman had my mobile arm in a lock. I couldn't move. Edmund looked at me with a face that figured pound, euro and dollar signs.

'Don't squeeze too hard,' he said. 'I want her alive for a bit longer.'

24

At Sea

It was like a Wild West film with the sheriff bursting into the saloon in the nick of time to save the heroine from kidnap by the baddies. Only it was Bruce Everton with several burly seamen, and he was followed by Dr Judith Skinner, her face ashen.

My throat was released and I fell back, coughing, gasping for breath. It was all happening so fast. But I was alive, just about.

Edmund seemed to shrink behind his desk. Bruce Everton went straight over to him and said something which I couldn't hear. Everywhere was noise. There was another commotion as the woman was restrained behind me. She was putting up a struggle.

Judith clutched my good arm. 'Have you taken any of those tablets I prescribed for you, Casey? You know, the antibiotics?'

'No,' I said, shaking my head. 'Sorry, but I forgot . . . '

'Thank goodness. Helen gave you the wrong pills. I've only just spotted the mistake. She gave you some Warfarin which I only keep in case we get a patient with a blood clot or heart valve disorder.'

'And is that dangerous?'

'You'd start bleeding in a few days. Eyes first, nose, internally. Very nasty.'

It was then that I recognized the woman's voice from behind me, the owner of the muscular arm across my throat, pressing down on my larynx. It was Helen, the chief nurse, the strong woman in Edmund's life.

She was the garrotter with a stick and a silk scarf. It had been a chain of blackmail and murders. He did the extortion and she did the extinction if the victims refused or threatened to expose them. They were an unlikely couple. One weak, the other strong.

Helen was standing there, heaving, glaring at me with hatred.

'I could have been like you, in a fancy uniform with fancy clothes,' she snarled. 'Only they turned me down. Too big and too ugly for the entertainment department, only they didn't quite put it like that. They said it was something to do with attitude.'

'I'm sorry if you wanted my job,' I said, forcing the words out. 'But you've rather blown it now.'

Bruce was removing the microphone from my bra strap and the recorder from my waist. 'You should go now, Casey,' he said. 'You need a strong coffee and a brandy. Go and sit down. I'll get a statement from you later.'

'A statement?'

'It all has to be written down. Statutory police procedure. More for the paper mountain.'

'But she was going to kill me. Twice. The wrong pills and then half-throttling me.'

'I know. We saw and heard everything that was happening, but you are safe now. Leave it all to us.'

'Saw?'

360

'There's a tiny camera fixed in the corner, up there. We didn't tell you in case you looked at it. You might have given it away.'

I saw a familiar face in the doorway. It was Captain Wellington. He was opaque with rage and shock. He took in the situation immediately.

'Lock them up,' he said. 'I'll arrange for their deportation ashore immediately. We can delay our departure from St Lucia. We can easily make up the time overnight.'

'I'd like reinforcements from shore police,' said Bruce.

'You'll get it.'

Judith was ushering me out. She did not look at Helen. She could not hide her disappointment and outrage.

'She was going to kill me,' I said again. I was like a broken record.

'Don't think about it, Casey. Let's check you out first. You might have a few bruises.'

'I'd rather have a brandy,' I said.

'You deserve a double.'

It was the nicest thing anyone had said

for days. I was emerging from the nightmare. Perhaps Bruce would explain it all to me when he had time. I'd gathered that Edmund blackmailed passengers and maybe even members of the crew. Helen helped him gather evidence for blackmail. She would obviously pass on any snippets of gossip from the medical centre. And she had access to medical histories.

Then if any blackmail victim became difficult and threatened to report the situation, she was the one with the stick and the scarf. Edmund would be too squeamish. Helen had probably trashed Tracy's cabin, some sort of twisted revenge.

Tracy had discovered Edmund's after-hours activities and had to be silenced. Lorna Fletcher had enough spirit to resist his blackmail. Edmund wouldn't have known that Mr Fletcher had been in the police force. But Sally Newman was a mystery. We knew nothing about her or the circumstances of her death.

Then I remembered what Romanoff had told me. He had a wife in Moscow.

Edmund had tried to blackmail him and Tracy found out, threatened to go to the captain and that was enough to sign her eternal silence.

I didn't want to go to Judith's cabin or to the medical centre. I had a severe case of claustrophobia. No small spaces, please, and nowhere that would remind me of recent events. We went instead to the Bridge Bar which was usually quiet at this time of day.

The only person there was Ted Sullivan, looking his old self.

'Allow me,' he said. 'Two double brandies, ladies? You both look as if you need them.'

'And some coffee, please,' said Judith hastily. 'One of us still has to work.'

'Both of us still have to work,' I reminded her. 'There's this evening's show to introduce. Pierre has been drinking all day. I doubt if he'll be fit for it.'

'He can hold his drink remarkably well,' said Judith. I didn't mention her sister. I was not supposed to have heard that quarrel.

'I won't join you,' Ted went on. 'I have a feeling you ladies have a lot to talk about. Perhaps another time, Doctor? Would you care for a late night drink?'

Judith looked slightly disconcerted. She didn't get many late night dates. 'Thank you, Mr Sullivan. That would be very nice. How are you feeling now?'

'Top of the world,' he said, raising his glass.

'We never found out who spiked your bottle of water.'

'I shouldn't bother. It was that mean-faced John Fletcher who couldn't stand the sight of me, especially when I made his wife laugh. He offered me a water bottle in the departure lounge before we boarded the tenders to go ashore. Said I might need it on the rough trip. Nice little thing, Lorna. We got on rather famously.'

The brandies and coffees arrived together. I needed the coffee more than I needed the alcohol. I was surprised to see that my hands were still shaking. Mentally I was coming out of the shadows, but my body didn't agree.

'I'm going to recommend to Head Office that you are relieved of all duties,' said Judith, stirring in rather a lot of sugar.

'I seem to have heard that before,' I said. 'Pierre suspended me recently.'

She ignored me. 'You've been on a roller coaster of physical maltreatment and the body can only take so much. There was the hurricane, then the raiders and being shot and now this attempted assault. You need rest and recuperation. I think you should fly home from Barbados, our next port of call.'

'It would certainly be wonderful to get home,' I said with longing. 'My own bed, my own things, my own view.'

'You are going to have some bruising,' she added, eyeing my throat with professional briskness. 'Wear a scarf or something.'

I shuddered. 'No scarf, thank you.'

'Sit there and enjoy your coffee,' she said. 'I'll be back in five minutes.'

I did as I was told. There was a faint background of music in the bar and it was enough to almost send me to sleep. I was sleep deprived. Small flakes of heaven seemed to fall on to me, lulling me in to peace. It was easy to imagine myself miles away, anywhere — a desert island, perhaps in the Seychelles — with waves washing a gentle shore.

'It might have been longer than five minutes.'

'I've arranged everything,' she said, sitting back down. 'You're flying back from Barbados, business class, so you'll have enough leg room for those long legs. That is, if your arm continues to heal. If not, then it'll be an air ambulance.'

'No way,' I said emphatically. 'I'm not going home in an air ambulance.'

'And I've arranged for you to have an escort, someone to carry your suitcase, that sort of thing. Wheel you about.'

'I refuse to be wheeled about.'

But I could not be really angry with Judith. She was being incredibly kind, organizing my departure, smoothing everything over. I only had to survive the night. We'd be in Barbados tomorrow morning.

'Are we ever going to find out who shot

at me with a sawn-off shotgun?'

'Not unless they confess. My bet is that it was Edmund. He thought you were getting too close. He wanted to put you out of action for a good while. If it had hit a bone, your injury would have been more serious. But he missed, of course.'

Home. I was flying home tomorrow. I could hardly believe it.

★　★　★

We went as a party to the spectacular show that evening. There was Judith and Ted Sullivan, Daniel Webster and Romanoff Petrik, Debbie and Gary, Fiona and Angus MacDonald. Bruce Everton had gone, with his detainees. I barely had time to say goodbye. It was a distant wave from the deck.

We'd shared a table at dinner and we were now ready to be entertained.

I wore a dress I hadn't worn before. It had to have one airing before its return to the suitcase. It was a vintage cream satin dress, circa 1935, cut on the bias, that folded round like layers of whipped cream and still didn't crease. It had a label from a fashion house in Paris, long since gone. My sling blended.

Daniel cut up my food for me. Romanoff poured the wine. Gary had to leave early. He had work to do, he said.

It was a great show, plenty of singing and dancing and an imported comedy duo that were really funny. But the star of the show was Pierre Arbour. Unintentionally, of course. He came on to present the show, smoothtalking the introduction, hogging the microphone for a full five minutes. Some of his words were slurred.

Then as he turned to leave, he tripped. No one could see what he tripped over. I think it was his own feet. He sprawled across the stage and when some stage hands rushed on to help him up, blood was pouring from his nose, all down his immaculate white ruffled shirtfront.

To add to his discomfiture and the amusement of the audience, he had split his tight trousers. And his bikini pants were the same colour as his gushing blood.

Debbie winked at me. 'Gary said that

he'd had more than one too many,' she said. 'Gary was counting, but Pierre wasn't. Of course, Pierre never counts when someone else is paying.'

He would never live it down. His career was as good as over.

25

Barbados

At six a.m., the *Countess Aveline* sounded 'stand by below' three miles from our berth at Barbados. Fifteen minutes later, I heard the pilot coming on board to navigate us through the breakwaters to our berth.

We were not far from Bridgetown with all its shops and Cheapside Market and the Careenage, the busy inner harbour. Everyone had to see Trafalgar Square and Nelson's life-size bronze statue. It was only a short taxi ride into the town. Before the huge new commercial docks were built, one could have walked it.

A stewardess came to help me pack. I had slept well after the show. Very well. I had closed the show amid loads of applause and cheers, and apparently some of it had been for me. I thought it was for the dress.

I was halfway in to my periwinkle-blue casual trouser suit, when there was a knock at my cabin door. My head was submerged in the bloused top. I heard Judith's voice outside.

'Your medical escort has arrived, Casey. You'll be all right now on the flight home. There's someone here to take care of you.'

'Ask her to wait outside a moment,' I said, struggling. 'I'm not quite dressed.'

But the door opened slowly. I felt my skin prickle. I knew who it was before he came in. It was that wonderful sixth sense that would play forever in my mind. He stood in the doorway just as I remembered him, tall and good-looking. He was smiling that funny smile and watching my mouth. The desire to touch him was so strong that I had to try and distance myself.

'How do you like your morning?' asked Dr Samuel Mallory, fresh from the medical centre of the *Countess Georgina*. I found out later that she had been cruising the Caribbean, close by us.

'I'm beginning to like it very much,' I

croaked. My throat still hurt. 'Do you still want me to call you Sam?'

'Sam will do fine.'

'I've bought you a wooden duck,' I added.

'It's what I've always wanted.'

THE END